SUPERIOR
PASSAGE

A SEAFARING TALE BY
RICHARD T. COLEMAN

PAGE PUBLISHING, INC.
New York, NY

First originally published by Page Publishing, Inc. 2019

ISBN 978-1-64424-339-8 (Paperback)
ISBN 978-1-64424-340-4 (Digital)

Printed in the United States of America

1

THERE IS A line drawn on a map that separates a portion of Canada from northern Michigan at the easternmost end of the massive lake named Superior. This line is drawn along the banks of the St. Marys River that meanders from Lake Superior to the shores of Lake Huron to its south. Superior's waters flow down along the Canadian-American borders toward the southeast and are equally received by Lake Huron and Lake Michigan.

Huron and Michigan are Indian names that somehow ended up on maps that were drawn by the white men who explored this country first. The name Superior, however, was originally le Lac Superieur, a tribute by the French to the massive beauty, size, and majesty this lake possesses. Superior, with its 32,483 square miles of surface, is the largest inland body of water by volume in the world, and aside from the St. Louis River at its western end, the St. Marys River is the largest and only outlet; otherwise all the rivers and creeks from its adjoining lands flow into this Great Lake.

I managed to make my way to the mouth of the St. Marys River on my way to Lake Superior back in the year 1937. I sailed and motored my thirty-six-foot sloop up the St. Marys River and through the locks that slow the flow of Superior's waters into Lake Huron. The river drops in excess of twenty feet in its trip from Lake Superior to Lake Huron. The two days of motoring and locking through the St. Marys River had given me a look at a new country that was exciting and seemed incredibly foreign to me.

Nowhere in the eastern United States had I seen such a wide array of plants and animals in such a confined area. Every inch of that country abounds with life. Most outstanding of all, though, are the friendly and mysterious Chippewa people of the northern region. All my experiences with these generous and happy people were good.

Though these were citizens of my own country, the people of this region were different in so many ways from the people where I grew up on Cape Cod in Massachusetts. Almost all my northern acquaintances were pleasant, that is, save one soul whom I am sure must have escaped from hell itself, but there will be more of this tale later.

My love of exploring the world that is accessible by sea had taken me to Lake Superior, and the adventure I hoped to find, I did find. I narrate this tale with the help of a ship's log that I kept on a daily basis, as is the duty of any captain worth his salt. The pages of this log, from the time I was introduced to the vastness and beauty of this Great Lake to when I left the region, are filled with an adventure that brought together all the elements a human could hope to endure. The adventure I will relate to you, leaving nothing out that would by chance make the author look less humble or, for that matter, less foolish.

* * *

I began this trip in early June of the same year, leaving my loving wife, Emma, waving goodbye from the little dock behind our house in Chatham on the southern shore of Cape Cod in Massachusetts. Dear Emma had waved goodbye from that spot many times in the past, and I remember her flapping her little rose-embroidered apron in the air at me that day, like she was shaking something like muffin crumbs out of it, while half-smiling and waving goodbye. I knew that inwardly she feared for my safe return, not knowing for sure if she would ever see me again.

Emma is as hardy a woman as ever there was. The daughter of a fisherman, she was no stranger to seeing her men go off to sea. The day I left, her smile was betrayed by her eyes, which showed a sorrow of uncertainty. I knew we would be together again, though life for her would surely be harder to cope with without me to help her with her chores and provide her with human company. Her days would not be tortured, though, by the presence of a restless seafaring man pacing and rambling about from the lack of adventure. She knew I had to go, and though she protested only slightly, I knew she would grow weary of my absences, but go I had to anyway.

My first leg of this particular adventure was an easy sail from the Cape northeast, out to the edge of the Grand Banks of the North Atlantic. The vast sea opened to welcome me as the land disappeared behind. Out in the open sea, my whole being felt the comfort of familiar surroundings as the great rolling waves rolled my precious vessel gently over its swelling liquid hills.

I indulged my senses in the endlessness of the sea with its attendants, such as the sea birds that curiously approach or the great sea turtles who lift their heads to look when I sail by and the flying fish that dart away in surprise at my arrival. There is a never-ending array of creatures inhabiting this place, some large, like the shy Beluga whales and the elusive Narwhale of the Canadian shores, and the occasional Petrel who might find a rest from its flight somewhere on your deck.

There is always a period of time that it takes a seafarer to acclimate back to the feel and smells of the enormous bounty of ocean water that surrounds him. With a good wind pouring in from far off in the east, my boat settled on a course that would take me effortlessly to a place where I had been many times before—the Grand Banks of Nova Scotia. I settled in and kicked back on my cockpit bench, feeling the sea tugging at my hand on the tiller as the sea slithered beneath my boat and past the rudder, leaving it behind in a bubbling, swirling trail.

There along the Grand Banks I sailed to within sight of the fleet of great schooners that harvests the codfish along those shoal waters every summer. I actually sailed to within shouting distance of Captain Ned Radebaugh's schooner, *Tarmella*, where I hove to, and we exchanged kind words between old friends. We had sailed many sea miles together when we were youths, and it was good to see him.

Ned Radebaugh now owned a seventy-two-foot-long two-masted schooner with a crew of nine men and seven longboats. All his boats were out fishing as I approached, tending their long lines and fishing for their very existence, not to mention the pride of their sturdy little ship. They all hoped they could fill their hold with salted cod early on and beat the other schooners back to port to fetch the best of the prices paid to the first in of this rugged bunch.

Ned wanted me to come aboard his schooner and have a toast to old times with him, but my course was set, and I knew that I would have to keep to my schedule in spite of my desire to join him. Many years of sailing single-handed had taught me how to plan my trip so that I could find time to sleep in the vast openness of the sea where there were few dangers of running into land or ship. I bid old Ned goodbye until another time when we could toast each other and share old stories without care for duty.

From these bountiful banks, I steered a northwesterly direction up through the Cabot Strait to the mouth of the St. Laurence River, off the coast of Quebec, in Ontario, Canada. That river would take me past the great cities of Quebec and Montreal and into the Great Lakes of North America. From there I would find my way into Lake Huron and Lake Eire, then past the city of Detroit, and north beyond cities and civilization.

Rising early to search the predawn horizon for a glimpse of lights that would mark the approach to the Cabot Strait and then the St. Laurence River was a familiar practice for me. I watched the old schooner *Tarmella* drifting in the light airs, hove to with fore and mizzen sails reefed to the wind. I knew that life was good and felt the lights of Cabot Straits would come much too soon and spoil my pleasant sail.

My knowledge of the sea and its ways came to me early in life, taught to me by my grandfather, Patrick Murphy, for whom I was named, but most people I know call me by my childhood name, Shotty Murphy. My entire youth was spent on the sea, and it was said that I could stand on a rocking deck without holding on before I could even talk. Everything I know about the sea I learned from my grandfather. What he knew about the sea he had learned the hard way, through hard times. What I learned from him was all good.

My grandfather was a great sailor and had stood on the deck of many a tall ship. He began his sailing career in the early eighteen hundreds, sailing from Ireland as a young boy, serving as a cook's helper, and then working his way up not only to captain but to owner of a ship and then the owner of a company that owned many ships. His stories never ceased to amaze me, and they led me to read about other great mariners, like Sir Francis Drake, the incredible exploits of Admiral Lord Nelson, and the likes of the amazing men such as William Bligh and William Kidd.

Because Grandfather was Irish, he avoided being constricted into the British Navy, which was a common practice in his youth. The costly wars between Great Briton and France or Spain called for as many able-bodied seamen as the British could find or muster, as they would say. But my grandfather had the good fortune to be involved at that time in the merchant fleet that did the commerce that kept the trade between the fledgling independent States of America and England alive in those days.

By the time he was in his thirties, he had already cut a wide swath and had many friends in ports all over the world. Irishman or not, he kept a portrait of Admiral Lord Nelson hanging over his chair so all that stood in front of his desk, stood at the feet of Lord Nelson, the greatest seaman there ever was, as I was told by Patrick Murphy, who always stood when he mentioned the man's name.

The salt in my blood was sea salt. Any soul that went to sea in search of something that was beyond their own backyard excited my senses and caused my mind to wander toward the adventures they had. Books about the French explorers, fur traders, and Jesuit priests who worked their way west through North America in search of a new country and its wealth had captured my attention and convinced me that I would someday explore their paths. The grit in these men's souls was like a magnet to my dreams of new frontiers and places never seen. Many hours were spent dreaming that I might have been lucky enough to be one of these great adventures. How I wished I had discovered a new world on my own.

As fortune would have it, my grandfather had accumulated great wealth, which made it possible for me to travel and explore without the burden of working for a living. Though I never obtained the stature of that good man, he did make sure that I spent most of my youth in the rigging of one or another of his big ships, working side by side with the common seamen, who had no idea that my grandfather was the man that provided them with their pay.

Over the years I worked my way up from an ordinary seaman to a mate, to first mate, and then eventually to captain, and I held each position proudly. Alas, I was forced to quit the sea after Patrick Murphy died at the ripe old age of ninety-one. Being at sea was all I knew, but I was called to another duty, one that would put me ashore and that I could not refuse.

Reluctantly I agreed to help my dear mother run the substantial shipping business my grandfather and his brother, Frank Murphy, had established in the great city of Boston. From our land-based office, which occupied a very large warehouse, I was forced into a daily routine of endlessly moving paper from one desk to another. It was there that I was first introduced to things like telephones and adding machines. Stacks of paper never left my sight. Every time I would finish one stack and get it off my desk, it would only be replaced by someone whose only job was to put it there.

Uncle Frank Murphy had become feeble of body and mind long before his enterprising brother had died, so he was relegated to a corner office, where he could gaze daily out his window and watch the ships in their comings and goings. In the old Irish tradition, it was I that set about doing his work. He was a good man, and though I never got used to a steady deck, I was glad to do the old gent's work for him.

After ten years of hard work and many funerals, including putting Sina Murphy, my dear mother, to rest, I sold that thriving business and went back to the sea, but this time to the tune of my own drumbeat. Selling the family business was a big decision for us, but I knew my days inside of buildings were done. Wearing shoes and ties and suit coats had made me as nervous as a bug on a dance floor.

The whole time I was consigned to work, the sea had beckoned my barefoot lust for spray and foam.

Every single land-locked day had brought the dream of freedom from doors and roads and walls and ceilings. Though my tasks were simple and a good life was my fate, the walls held no fascination for me. Give me salt and sun! I have always felt that my last day of gainful employment was my first day of true and untethered freedom.

It is true, though, that my early years of seafaring were fruitful indeed, and truly they provided me with the knowledge of the sea that worked its way from my mind to my very soul. Every day I spent on land, however, was a day of anxiety, filled with a longing to hear the sounds that are only created by the wind and waves. Warm or cold, sunshine or gloom, I loved the sea and the boats that plied the seas. The sea was my life. A farmer had his fields, the trucker had his roads, a rancher lived on and loved the range, and for me the great seas of this world were mine alone.

Every wall of the Wilburn Murphy Shipping Company office was covered with pictures of great ships and small boats of character. Each one was rich in its own history, and each one served to keep my dreams of buying a fine boat for myself alive. That single thought became the filler in every idle thought. I designed the boat I wanted over and over in my mind, day after day. There was nothing I had overlooked in my dreams, and upon retiring from the working world, I was ready. The day that I cleaned out my office was the last day that dreaming about sailing my own boat was all I could do. That was the day my dreams started to become a reality.

It was not long before I had settled on what it was I wanted in a boat. I would have one built for me, and it would be the solid form of so many hours of letting my mind wander through every conceivable function and form the boat could have. This boat was my dream. A dream I would make come to life, by god, and it would be mine to love and care for until death do us part. That boat did become reality, and she was every part of me that I had hoped she would be and more.

God, in his infinite wisdom, has created all wondrous things, it is true, but amongst those things of wonder, the bond he gave to a man and his boat must surely be the best thing ever. The love I had for my boat could only be described as true and enduring. My boat's name is *Nattily Ann*, and she served me faithfully without fault or failure through everything that was ever thrown her way. Never did she fail me, though unfortunately the opposite is not so true. To my great shame, I let her down, and I hope that this story may help set that unfortunate circumstance straight.

Nattily Ann was built out of oak and cedar at Boxer Boat Works in Duxbury, Massachusetts, on the shore of Cape Cod. The builder of this great boat was a gentleman named James Boxer, and even though he had built over twenty boats and had a reputation as a builder of good boats, the Great Depression of the late twenties and early thirties was affecting him. By the time I arrived at his shop in the fall of 1930, the winter of '31 promised to be a slow one, so Boxer was glad to schedule this boat building project. The workers of Boxer's yard rejoiced at the prospect of work, and the air was full of anticipation.

James Boxer was an uncommonly friendly man with an extreme talent for building strong boats, as it turned out. My wife's father owned a thirty-foot fishing boat that was built by Boxer, and I had become greatly impressed with it, so I commissioned Boxer to build my boat on the specifications which I had drawn up myself. A thirty-six-foot gaffed rigged sloop would be perfect for my needs.

She would be easy to single-hand with plenty of rig for carrying a lot of sail in the light summer airs. She would be built strong enough to withstand an encounter with ice, if need be, and fast enough to carry me far. The drawings I had made showed her a tad beamier than the style at the time, but I preferred the buoyancy that would give her, though I might lose some speed for it. The drawings gave little idea of what Boxer saw in his mind. I had no skill as a lofter of boats, but as it turned out, Boxer certainly did.

Boxer's son, Aaron, also had a talent, and his finish work in the cabin would have felt at home even in the finest hotels. Carefully sanded exotic-looking woods brought life and texture to what would, on most boats, be considered dull and drab. The wood used in the construction of this vessel was gathered from the local forests, and most had been stored in heated sheds for one whole winter to slowly squeeze out the moisture. The only wood that was imported was cedar for the hull that was harvested from America's great western forests.

This cedar possessed the finest, tightest grain I had ever seen. It was of a strong, light quality that would swell evenly when exposed to the sea, making the planks press hard against the tar-soaked cotton laid between each seam. A mixture of thick white lead paint and copper powder was pressed tightly into the cracks on top of the cotton so water leakage would never be a problem. Then the bottom was painted with copper-powder-soaked paint to keep the marine growth at bay.

The frames that held the planking together and shaped the hull were all hand-sawn and shaped out of large white oak tree trunks. Each frame was at least three inches square, and only a few were forced into shape by heating them with steam and bending them onto a jig. The deck beams were made of the same oak and showed a wonderful pattern of grains to enhance the interior decor. I myself was involved in the hunt for the proper black ash trees, ones that possessed the perfect crooks and crotches growing between the trunks and the branches, which would be sawn into the braces that joined the hull frames tightly to the deck beams. Once sanded and oiled, their luster was not to be matched by any other wood. *Nattily Ann*'s stem, keel, and horn timbers were hewn out of the same fine oak logs but were massive, sometimes in excess of six inches square. In all our seaward treks, I never feared for *Nattily Ann*'s strength.

The hull was finished with a large oak rub-rail and a one-inch half-round bronze strip that was mortised into the rub-rail the full length of the boat's sheer. We installed a four-inch cap rail on top of a three-inch toe rail that helped keep things on deck from slipping overboard whenever the boat would be swept by a wave. The rail was oak as well, but this oak was of the black variety, which I felt had a better resistance to the sun and weather and would hold paint better if I became tired of oiling and varnishing the full length of rail on either side of the boat's deck.

The deck itself was laid with local white pine the same way the planking was made water-tight, with oakum and red led putty, and then covered with heavy canvas and white lead-based paint to keep the moisture out. The pine deck would be lighter in weight but strong enough to resist any pounding from the sea or an accidental anchor dropped on it.

All in all, the marriage of the various woods, paints, and varnish, with bright shining ports, cleats, and other hardware that was made of soft bronze gave *Nattily Ann* a look of beauty mixed with a strength that could not be denied. Her decks, planks, and roofing were all fastened with heavy bronze nails and screws that never show streaks of rust, as might be seen on the hulls of lesser boats.

Even her chain pipes were made of bronze as well as her anchor windlass and scuppers. Truly, the only iron to be found on this prized vessel is the galvanized kedge anchor with its half-inch-thick galvanized anchor chain and the galvanized plates to secure the rigging. No expense was spared in her construction, and without a doubt, the extra expenditure was well worth it.

Because of the need to navigate rivers and locks, I had Boxer fit a brand-new two-cylinder, fifteen-horsepower Red Wing gasoline motor in *Nattily Ann*. Although not overly powerful, the motor was reliable and gave me the push I needed on windless days or in a contrary current which might want to keep me from going in some fickle inlet or another.

We stocked enough spare parts to ensure that if almost anything went wrong with the Red Wing, I would be in a position to repair the engine myself. There was also enough extra canvas stored on board that if the motor failed, I always had plenty of sail material to sail the world without it. A brand-new bolt was stored under my amidships bunk for safekeeping and would prove to be a priceless possession in days to come.

I have heard from more than one source on more than one occasion that Boxer had bragged that *Nattily Ann* might have been the best boat he had ever built. I would certainly not argue that point. A fine boat, like a fine painting, should be there for all to enjoy for its grace and beauty. The pride of ownership is greatly enhanced when the object one owns possesses beauty beyond the norm, and indeed, *Nattily Ann* is one of those possessions.

It seemed like just yesterday that I stood in the cool spring air with my wife by my side, watching as the boat shop crew pushed Nattily Ann out of the shed and onto the ways that sloped down into the river's edge. We named the boat *Nattily Ann* after our only two children, and the name seemed perfect for this boat's sleek, feminine charm. A cable was attached to her cradle, and an old make-and-break motor was thrown into gear, while we watched as she lurched forward and slowly jerk down the ways and into the water of Duxbury Sound.

At first it looked like she was going to sink by her stern as she slid into the water, but as the cable pulled the cradle further out, she began to free herself. Soon, there before my eyes was the most beautiful boat I had ever seen afloat. Sitting at dockside with her new white painted hull and red boot stripe, it was hard for me to take my eyes off her. From the tip of her six-foot bowsprit, along her smooth flowing sheer, to the cap of her aft rail, she demonstrated more thoroughbred than any boat I had ever seen before. I was sure that the great naval architect Nathaniel Herreshoff himself would have been envious indeed.

It took over a week and the work of three men to put the tall spruce mast in and bend on the new canvas sails, but since that day, hardly a week has gone by without me setting her free from her mooring and taking her out for a run. Anyone who has owned a boat, no matter what the size, has found a life to exist in its wood, paint, varnish, and canvas. The vessel somehow becomes an extension of the skipper's body and mind, and the two work together to create the most beautiful marriage between man and machine I have ever known.

A brand-spanking-new boat, especially one of your own design, is cause for a pride that may make the trip to heaven a somewhat rocky road. I am sad to say that my infatuation with that boat at first caused me to neglect almost everything else in my life, except my wife, of course, who found a love for *Nattily Ann* in her heart also. She spent many hours with us, fitting and refitting the rigging, and she was responsible for having the sails properly done. Her knowledge of the sea and boats was invaluable in turning out a very seaworthy vessel. Though she had a tender touch in the home, she was as tough as any fisherman who tugged a net when she went to sea, which she had done with her father every summer of her young life.

From the time I commissioned *Nattily Ann* to this day, *Nattily Ann* and I have taken many a run, and most of them found adventure. Unfortunately, the particular run through the Great Lakes that I am telling about here was almost the last run for both of us. Only fate intervened to save us both from what would have been an unknown demise. Though times have changed in the years that have passed, and now there is the common use of ship-to-shore radios and radio navigation, nothing of that sort was available to me on this trip, and aside from the stars, some rudimentary maps, and a good compass, I had little to aid in my navigation.

Whole worlds were discovered with little more than knowledge of the stars, so don't get the idea that I'm complaining. I merely point out that, at the time of this story, any seaman afloat was pretty much at the mercy of the wind and the sea. I was a lone seaman with my trusted boat for a companion; like the range rider's horse, my boat was always part of me, and I trusted her with my life.

W ALKING THE STREETS of Sault Sainte Marie, Michigan, with two paper sacks of fresh provisions, I carefully navigated the narrow breakwater out to my waiting boat. Early morning mist was lightly falling, and the boardwalk to my boat gave little sound footing. I remember that moment well, because the jump from pier to boat almost sent me headlong into the water. I laughed when I thought that the most dangerous part of sailing the world was boarding my own dock-bound boat.

Sault Sainte Marie is one of two bustling little seaports on a river, each in a different country, both sporting the same name. They are settled on the northernmost part of the river that connects Lake Superior to Lake Michigan and Lake Huron and the rest of the world, for that matter. They have seen everything from big freight canoes filled with brightly clad paddlers, to large oceangoing freighters pass in a daily procession, moving every sort of cartage to and from every corner of the planet. These two little bergs have heard almost every language spoken by man, and yet they are as remote a place as one could ever find on this earth.

I felt a pioneering spirit existed there, and I bristled with the feel of adventure. This was truly part of a great frontier. As early as the sixteen hundreds, this was the convergence of two totally different cultures. Traders and trappers from Imperial France found their way here, and after doing so, they found the local Ojibwa to be a friendly and peaceful group, willing to barter and trade. It was a natural portage, and the Indians had a wonderful ability to build big canoes from the local forests. Many of the forty-foot freight canoes were built right on the banks of what is now known as the St. Marys River.

I found the sight of these canoes, still plying the river waters filled with families and freight packs, exhilarating. I could only imagine the scene had changed little for the Chippewa through those many years. Their festive clothing and rugged features showed well that they were people of the land. I envied the simplicity of their simple existence.

After stowing my provisions in their proper place, I cranked over the Red Wing motor and headed out for the open water. After a short run up St. Marys River, out into Whitefish Bay, I pointed northwest for what would be a short trip that would put me on a dock in the makeshift harbor at Whitefish Point, about a six-hour run. From there I would have a clear shot into Lake Superior's open water. After a good night's sleep, it was my hope to leave Whitefish Bay before sunrise and sail all day until I would sight a light that marked the channel entrance to Munising at Grand Island, sometime shortly after midnight. This would be my first leg out in the big lake and the first day of a two-month cruise.

The day went well as I encountered a smart breeze from the southwest, making good time and arriving at White Fish Harbor well before sundown. There, I made the acquaintance of several old fishermen who were engaged in laughter and chatter while mending their nets. They shared their strong tea with me and showed me some charts they had of these waters. Most were copies of government surveys, like the ones I already had, but many footnotes had been added by the fishermen to show where to go in case of foul weather. They had also marked some shoals that were definitely not printed on my charts. I copied down everything I felt would be pertinent to my safety.

These were weathered men, six of them in all, who went out in open boats to set their nets for herring, whitefish, and trout to send off to market. One rowed, others sailed, and some motored their boats far offshore to drop nets and return in a few days to retrieve their catch. I could see firsthand that there were many hardships and much work to make a living like this, but I knew that if they were given the choice to do something other than fish, they would still fish.

That evening, going over the charts in preparation for my next leg, I made this second and final entry for the day:

> 20:15 August 4; there is a light offshore breeze from southwest with seas running one foot. Local knowledge of reefs and shoals obtained. Provisions stowed for early morning departure. Aside from the mosquitoes, I find this to be a most pleasant place to lie. The good people shared their meal of chicken and beans cooked on an open fire. Leftovers were wrapped in newspaper and given to me for my trip. They were very nice people indeed.

The next morning's sky was showing a pink glow as I secured my dock lines on board. There was no need to worry that the sound of my motor would wake any fishermen, because they had all left the dock well before my coming up on deck. With no wind blowing, I headed out and followed the stern light of the last boat on his journey around the point to the open waters of Lake Superior.

The morning chill was washed down with fresh hot coffee I poured out from my thermos jug. With my arm over the tiller and my eye on the sunrise, the sound of the engine drifted slowly through my mind and over the water toward the shore that was growing smaller and smaller. Each boat found its own designated route, and shortly we were all left to ourselves, heading out over the smooth rolling waters of this massive Great Lake Superior.

Just as I had suspected, the wind began to rise shortly after sunrise. I fastened my tiller and went below to find my light air jib sail. Expecting a day of light summer wind, I chose to use my big jib that was cut from some lighter canvas than any of the working sails. It was very large and held almost as much square footage as the main sail, which is no little sail. I dragged it forward, pulled it out from its bag, and hanked it on to the head stay. I fastened the jib halyard to its top and walked the port and starboard sheets back to the cockpit, making sure everything was outside of the rigging. With the security of knowledge, I hoisted the sail hand over hand until it was completely up, then secured the halyard around a belaying pin at the base of the mast. Turning to the main sail, which was always in place, I repeated the effort, and within a minute, both sails were aloft and flapping lazily as the motor drove us into the wind. Aft, into the cockpit, I turned off the motor and released the helm to run starboard so the sails could fill themselves and catch the wind.

Shafts of red, pink, and purple light reflected off the dark waters as *Nattily Ann* rose and dove gently over almost imperceptible swells. The comfort given by the absence of noise from the motor is like finding out that you had a headache because you realize that it is no longer there. This type of serenity adds time to one's life, I am quite sure.

As the sun rose slightly above the horizon, heating the air, the wind rose steadily and shifted more to the south. I veered off so that I had the wind off my port rail. Even though the Michigan shoreline I would be following was mostly sandy beaches and bottoms, it was always my practice to stay well off the coast when making long passages. There were a few places marked on my charts that I felt would be nice to explore, but if weather or wind were contrary, I was prepared to sail nonstop to the city of Duluth at the western end of the Lake Superior. I am as comfortable on my boat as I am anywhere else for my home is my boat and its home is the sea.

Fort Francis, Marquette, and Duluth were the only port cities large enough to have a ship chandlery or boat hauling facilities, if it turned out that there was a need. Duluth was my destination or, to be precise, thirty miles east of there at the Brule River, where the great French explorer Sieur Duluth found a way by which he could forage by canoe and foot to the spot on what is now the Mississippi River, where the capital of Minnesota, St. Paul, now stands.

West of there it was into the Great Plains that encompasses most of this country. On my way there I hoped I would be able to visit a group of islands called the Apostle Islands, to see the old set-

18

tlements at Madeline Island, Bayfield, and Ashland in Chequamegon Bay. The settlement at La Pointe on Madeline Island is the oldest outpost on the lake continuously occupied by white men. La Pointe was the home of the fur trading industry dating back to the sixteen hundreds, and many great pioneers and traders built homes and forts on the island during America's early history. The bay where these communities are settled has been ruled, one way or the other, by the French, the Spanish, the British, and the Americans.

All my plans for this exploration to the western end and back along the Canadian shoreline of Superior hinged on me being able to explore as much as possible, as fast as possible. I would have to leave this lake sometime before the weather turned foul, sometime in October. The fishermen at Whitefish Point had related stories about Superior's fall storms that made my neck bristle. There is a story, mythical or not, of the legendary Three Sisters. Giant waves that were born somewhere to the east and grew to be the size of a barn by the time they made it to western shores. It was said that these waves traveled close together in groups of three, and no ship or boat known had ever encountered them and survived to tell the story. The description given of these Three Sisters hit a skeptical ear, but the last thing I wanted was to encounter one of Superior's legendary storms.

I am not sure if my thoughts of storms were generated by an idle mind or whether it was the sight of ominous clouds far off in the west. I had settled into my usual routine and balanced my helm so I could slip below to brew up another pot of coffee. I was so happy to be able to just reach over the side of my boat and fill my empty pot with that fresh, clear, cold Lake Superior water. My little wood-fired stove heated the pot to a boil rapidly once I tossed a couple of sticks of charcoal on the glowing embers already there. Just the smell of coffee brewing brought warmth to my soul.

Back up on deck, I settled into my fresh cup of hot coffee, letting my eyes wander out toward the western sky. In my short absence to make coffee, the clouds had grown larger and much darker. Though many miles away, I could see the clouds were thick and dark, which usually meant they were full of rain. The bright sunlit tops of those clouds were very high, and they traveled uninterrupted from sky to sea. The turquoise green-blue of the lake contrasted starkly with the blackness of the approaching storm. I didn't much like what I was seeing. Assessing that the storm must have been quite a way off and probably was not a threat to me, I did what I always do anyway: plotted an alternate course. By the time I'd had my fill of coffee, I became aware that the waves were rising even though the wind had not appreciably risen in turn. This I could only attribute to the forthcoming storm being larger and slower moving than I had first thought. The morning had bought gentle waves that rose and fell only a foot or two, but without any noticeable increase in wind, the waves were now in excess of two feet. This, I felt, was strange, but then I had little knowledge of fresh water's habits.

Jumping down into the cabin and rolling out a chart on the table, I pressed it down and began to study it carefully. I noted in my log the time and my course.

> Two hundred ninety degrees, and the wind was west southwest at about ten knots. My position was approximately 85-30'n, 47-00'w, about 27 miles west of Whitefish Point.

I decided to alter course to the north and bear for a small island on the chart that had Caribou Island handwritten next to it. There were no details, but Johan Erickson, a ham-fisted, weather-beaten old-timer, had mentioned that he sometimes anchored there to wait out weather or wait for the fish to swim into his nets. It would be an easy run if needed, and I was in no hurry.

So I entered the time and new course and wrote a guess as to when I might sight Caribou Island. I altered my course forty degrees to the north and prepared for what I thought would be a six-hour run. As soon as she found her course, *Nattily Ann* relaxed a little, and I eased her sheets for a comfortable reach toward the north. Sometimes a mariner has to change his plans for comfort or safety, and in this case, both were considered. With a course more off the wind, I could hear the bow cutting through a wave and the occasional swish of the water rushing in a fall gently away from my bow. A slow roll like the rocking of a baby's cradle and the occasional warm gust of wind made this leg of the ride seem very pleasant indeed. I was sure that if the storm made it this far, I would be well north of it and out of harm's way.

It was then that hunger took notice of me and started me thinking about that chicken I had shared with the good people of Whitefish Point. Looking around, making sure that all was well, I went below for a snack. I rolled the paper full of chicken over my table and began to eat it, remembering the lady who had cooked the meal. She was very tall and large for a woman, not really fat, but at first I thought she might have been a man dressed in woman's clothes. She looked at me and caught me curiously staring at her as we sat around the fire. She was pretty, but she was very large for a woman, which caused me to reflect.

Twenty years previous I had encountered a village in South America where the women were all large and the men were, you might say, petite. It was a small harbor town in Brazil that had a good spring for our water stores, and the native men were very adept at making charcoal for our cook's stoves. I did much commerce with these good people over the years. One peculiar thing stood out to me from the first time we stopped there for provisions. The men and women seemed to have switched roles. The men did all the work, and the women seemed to enjoy the tribal customs that were normally allotted to men. We saw the women and children endlessly playing some sort of ball sport, kicking a crude grass-filled skin-covered ball around the yard, apparently attempting to keep it away from someone on the opposite side, while the men stayed at work and on the periphery. When the women and children were not playing, they seemed to enjoy simply lounging about and being served by the men.

We also observed that the men did the cooking as well as the cleaning and gathering of the wood for their fires. This sexual changeabout I attributed to the fact that, though the women were shapely and good-looking, they possessed strong torsos like men usually have, and the men were generally smaller, more the size of women. The amazing thing was that the women were, for the most part, very beautiful. Their beautiful black hair was always immaculate, and their clothing was ornate and colorful, unlike the men, who were dirty and mostly wore nothing more than loincloth.

On one trip I almost lost my first mate to one of those women, who, I must say, had a beauty that far exceeded the forest from whence she came. I have never seen a man so struck before in my life, and it took all the persuasion I had in me to wrench him from her. I am sure that he must still think about that woman every day of his life and regrets ever leaving that beautiful place.

There were four pieces of good-tasting chicken in that rolled-up paper on my table, and I ate every last one of them. After sucking the meat off each bone, I would stand up on the companionway steps and toss the remnants overboard, looking all around the horizon as I did so. When I had finished, I cleaned up my mess and sat down on my bunk to pick the chicken remnants from my teeth. Carving and whittling are hobbies of mine, and there were plenty of splinters lying around to stick in my mouth and pick at the stuck chicken.

The motion of my boat's gentle rolling caused the wonderful creaks and groans that are made as wood rubs and bends against wood. While listening to that sound and the sound of the water slapping and rushing past my hull, I laid back on my bunk to savor the soothing cacophony for a little while and rest while the recently consumed chicken found its way home to my stomach. There, with a pillow tucked under my head, rolling the wooden pick around on my lips, a daydream gently floated into my mind. Somehow the little daydream turned into a nap, and then a heavy, deep sleep got a firm hold on me.

3

To this very day I can remember the voice of my wife, Emma, calling to me through a sandy-colored haze, calling my name over and over as if she were trying to wake me up. I didn't want to wake up because the sound of her voice was so warm and pleasant, but wake up I did. A loud bang, or crack, like a cannon being shot off close to my ship dumped me out of my bunk and onto the floor. I scrambled to my feet, my heart pounding and racing from fright, and looked around the darkened cabin, trying to reconnect with some reality. Something had hit my boat or something had broken on it, and for a moment, I stood helpless to move away from my groggy sleep.

I raced up into the cockpit, where it was apparent how deep my slumber had really been. The sky above me was as black as coal, and lightning was flashing all around, striking the water less than a mile away. It was the crack of lightning that had woken me. The tiller was swinging wildly from side to side with the pressure of the sea, and my mainsail gaff was straining under the stress of a greatly increasing wind. I grabbed the tiller and looked down at my compass. I was heading almost due east! Suddenly I became aware that I was in quite a predicament. There was way too much sail up for this wind, and judging by the severity of the approaching storm, things were not going to get better anytime soon. A quick look down into the salon on the forward bulkhead, where the chronometer and barometer were hanging, told me the tale. I had slept for almost two hours!

More importantly, my barometer was showing me that the barometric pressure was as low as I had ever seen it. No telling where I was on the charts or how long the ship had steered herself to the east. All I knew was that I needed to get control of the situation quickly.

As if the storm wasn't enough to deal with, I became aware of a bigger problem. As I eased the main and jib sheets to run before the wind, off in the distance I could see land. The peaks of mountains or hills were stretched across the horizon as far as I could see. A quick search of my memory of the charts told me this could only be the Canadian shoreline, and that was definitely not good. Canada is known for its rocky and unforgiving shoreline in these parts. Storms just like this one have carved away almost all the sand and shore, leaving only rough, rocky landscapes. I would have to turn the boat around and sail right through the heart of this storm in order to gain as much sea room as I possibly could to stay clear of this menacing coast.

There was no time to change the giant headsail; the wind was pushing its sheets to their limits, and the seas had already gotten too rough to safely go forward to change the sail, which would require venturing out on the bowsprit now dipping deeply into the rolling surf. Reducing the size of the mainsail would only add pressure to the headsail, so I decided to chance it and get as much speed as I could in hopes of crawling toward the west and away from that evil shoreline. So harden up the sails I did, putting the tiller into the wind, and off into the fray we went. There was hardly a moment before the hard rain hit for me to pull on my oilskins and sou'wester rain hat, but somehow I did manage to get them on.

The fury sent by the edge of the storm made me fear for its center. Superior's waves were growing taller, and with every wave that hit me, there was another one frothing and boiling to replace it. It soon became apparent that going to the weather was not going to be easy at all, if indeed, it were possible at all. My little boat would almost stop dead every time a wave slapped her bow, and when I fell off the wind, a little to gain some speed, the waves felt like they were going to toss us right into the air. After half an hour, I hadn't even gotten into the center of the storm, and I was sure that I was being pushed backward toward the east in front of this powerful force. By now we were rising and falling six feet or more within seconds, and the tiller strained frantically from one direction to the other, constantly trying to pull itself out of my hands.

Superior is well-known for her November storms. They are legendary. But this storm had not read the calendar. This storm was not waiting for November; it was here now! I strapped on a safety harness and tied myself into a pad eye in the cockpit. The motion of the boat would alternately leave me in midair and then push me down hard on the cockpit bench. Just to hold the tiller took all my strength. I had been in many storms in my life at sea, but this one was meaner than any storm I'd ever seen in the Atlantic, where the waves got farther apart as the wind grew. Here it was the opposite!

There was no rest from the pounding, and I was getting worried. I never doubted my boat's ability to take this beating, but other doubts began to enter my mind. These waves were growing higher and coming at us relentlessly. Every ounce of wood, rope, and canvas was being tested to its limits, and I was almost helpless to do anything other than sit there fighting the tiller and watching what was unfolding before me. This would be some story to tell, I thought, should we survive this onslaught.

I began to think hard about the shoreline, but it was raining so profusely I could barely see my bow. *Nattily Ann* was taking a lot of water over her bow and at the same time dipping her rail under from the strain of too much sail. The sound of the wind and the lightning roaring at us was horrendous. Lightning flashed everywhere, sometimes so close it blinded me. If this storm lasted too much longer, I was afraid something bad was lying ahead, and encountering it would be inevitable.

Running a ship up on a sandbar in Honduras was the worst thing to ever befall me in my many years at sea, but the situation at hand had all the trappings of a real disaster. Even though my mast was made of strong fir pine, with all this sail up, there was a danger of it snapping in two. Prudence and fear fought in my head. Fear, I am sure, told me in no uncertain terms that this was the time that might be good to send out a little message to God: "Just want to say that I'm down here and things are getting a little tricky, so if you don't mind, could you just keep an eye on me for just a little while? Thanks."

Lifting my now-closed cabin hatch so I could see the ship's clock again, I was shocked to realize that I had been fighting this storm for over an hour. This knowledge sent my heart into a flutter as the slight pang of fear grew and rolled over me. How far had that shore been from me, and when did I actually sight it? Having no idea of where I was and no way to scout the chart for safe harbor, which I knew didn't exist, my mind set into a slight panic. I knew Caribou Island would have been way off to the west and north if I had been on that easterly course for too long. I had undoubtedly not made any progress to the west; I was actually being swept fairly rapidly to the east. This one fact did not bode well. The very last thing any mariner wants is an unknown shore creeping up on him. The worst thing that could befall a skipper, aside from an open sea collision, would be to ground his ship. Many a good ship, along with its cargo, has been lost to nothing less than the negligence of its captain.

One thing after another paraded through my thoughts. I knew I could not turn and run before the wind, for that would surely invite disaster. Neither could I reverse my course. I just had no idea where I was. All I could do, assuming my sails held out, was to ride out this storm and lick the wounds after the whole thing was over. After all, summer storms can't last that long, can they? No sooner did that thought cross my mind then a gust hit with such ferocity that the rail sank underwater, and water started to pour into my cockpit. I heard a loud crack and looked up just in time to see my jib sail rip longitudinally right through the middle. Only strong waxed thread in the seams had kept it from ripping completely into shreds.

That was a bad stroke of luck, but there was no way I could go forward and get that poor sail down. It was just too dangerous. Even if I crawled and strapped myself to the safety rail, the moment I let go of the tiller, the boat would probably broach and lay helpless to the breaking seas. The sail just had to fend for itself. Quartering these seas with an injured headsail and a rain-soaked gaff main was the best I could hope for. I thought of my fifteen horsepower motor, but even if I could start it, it would do little to improve the situation. At least quartering the seas gave me a little rest, and there wasn't so much strain on my rig, but I knew I was losing ground. I was well aware that for every wave *Nattily Ann* broke through, two more were there to push her backward.

Sitting there in water up to my ankles, staring into a blinding rain, I thought of the dream the voice of my wife had woken me from. It was a vague memory of lovely flowery fields and the sounds of birds, like we were on a picnic or some other warm summer activity. I listened for Emma's voice again, but that sound couldn't be found. I thought how sorry I was I hadn't written her from Sault Ste. Marie. I had written her only twice in the two months I had been absent, and that was not enough. I regretted the ease with which you could take another human for granted when you are with them, but now that I knew I could not tell Emma how fond I truly was of her, there was a deep and abiding longing to touch her little hand. I hoped, in that moment, that I would have the chance to tell her of my regrets.

A sudden loud snapping sound shook me from those thoughts. A shackle holding the mainsheet block had broken, sending my main boom on a leeward lurch. With line, shackle, block, and all jerked violently and almost being pulled right out of the deck. I could swear I heard the sound of wood cracking when the boom reached the end of the sheet and came to an abrupt stop. All I needed at that point was for the main boom to go adrift! I set about securing and repairing the damage while hanging on, working as best I could, wrestling one-handed, using the other hand to grasp onto anything that would help sustain my own life.

Then it happened! My fears became compounded. As I lashed the block to its mooring, I saw through a break in the rain, straight off my bow, a looming a black wall of rock towering high over a broken shore. It was too close for me to believe! A shocking wave of fear made my task fall from my hands as I stood up for a better vantage point. Shielding my eyes from the rain with an open hand, I could see that danger lay only a mile or so directly ahead! Without a moment's hesitation, I flung open my companionway door, jumped below, and opened the hatch to the engine room. Frantically tossing stowage away from in front of the hatch and fighting for footing, I uncovered my engine. I fumbled clumsily in the dark engine compartment for the crank to start the engine. My fingers found it right where I knew it would be, and I pushed the crank onto the flywheel, giving it a violent twist.

Then I remembered to pull out the choke and started to wind the crank again in hopes the engine would start at the first try. One, two, three cranks, and on the fourth turn, she popped to life, sputtered for a moment, and then quit. In my haste to start it, I had forgotten to turn on the gas valve. One, two, three, and on until she popped to life once again on the tenth crank. Precious time was slipping away. Fifteen horsepower was little against the fury of this storm, but anything that could be done to extricate us from this situation must be done right now! Fifteen horsepower be damned, it was all I had.

I stood back and straightened my back while wiping the sweat from my eyes with the back of my hand. Standing there on that rocking floor, watching, hoping she would continue running, I had my feet kicked right out from under me. I was thrown violently to the cabin floor, landing flat on my back and banging my head with a jolt that sent flashing lights and sparks floating around in my vision. We had hit something! My head was stinging with pain as I leapt up and jumped into the cockpit. Before I could assess the situation, before I could see what was going on, I was abruptly knocked to the floor once again. This time my boat lifted right up out from the water, listed violently to starboard, and did what seemed like a one-hundred-eighty-degree pirouette, before crashing back into the water.

Nattily Ann had hit an underwater rock. I was completely disoriented and confused! My bow was now facing the open lake, into wind and waves, with sails and booms flailing about wildly and me ducking to avoid the boom as it swept insanely from side to side. I thought that these sounds combined with the ferocious noise of the wind could only have been matched by sound of the gates of hell crashing in around me. Helplessly drifting backward with only moments before the wind would catch the bow again and turn *Nattily*

Ann on an uncontrolled plunge toward more rocks and into disaster, I tried to gather what consciousness I still had in me.

I began to sweat profusely and felt as if I would choke from lack of air. My head was ringing with pain, and I could feel warm blood running down my arm, where something sharp had torn at me in the melee. I ripped at my jacket until I found myself standing stripped to my undershirt and soaked to the bone. I desperately reached for the shift lever and thrust my sputtering engine into forward gear. While doing this, I momentarily looked over my shoulder and saw the fearsome sight of giant looming rock formations too close for me to comprehend. If there were to be an escape, it would be under engine power alone. I felt the lever engage the transmission, and there was a moment's relief as we lurched forward into the wind and caught some momentum. Then, suddenly and abruptly, the engine stopped again! My broken main sheet had fallen into the water and was grabbed up by the sucking motion of the propeller, wrapping the line around the shaft, freezing it hopelessly in place. Things could not get worse!

Faster than I could react, the wind grabbed *Nattily Ann*'s bow and started blowing it around to where the beam would be naked to the now breaking waves. Summoning all my thought power and strength, I swung the tiller hard over to port, putting the full force of the wind directly on my now fully extended mainsail. Sail, boom, and gaff thrust harshly up against the shrouds. If luck had any favors left for me, I would find some friendly bottom on which to drop anchor and ride out the rest of this nightmare. I was fearful that, with the main all the way out, my reaction time would be reduced by speed, but for some reason, speed was not there. Actually, *Nattily Ann* was rolling sluggishly and out of sync with the waves. This could mean only one thing; she was taking water!

My heart pounded as I lifted the cabin hatch. What my subconscious knew, but my hopes denied, I viewed below me. There I saw a mass of soggy flotsam swaying from side to side like some weird aquatic waltz, splashing up over my bunk, and then draining off it with a fall of water, dragging with it my simple possessions at the whim of the sea. My options were dwindling rapidly!

I spun around in haste, first looking at my deck then to the limited view of the rain-clogged horizon, every image etching on my mind. Over my cabin top was a small dinghy strapped upside down to the frame where it rested. There was little or no chance I could survive a row to some peaceful shore. Was there even time to prepare? Provisions, clothing, books, how, where, when? Waves were breaking over my foundering boat's deck and rolling past me toward an unseen shore, so I knew my time was very short.

Again, looking toward the phantom shore, there in the gloom, I could see something. Sheltering my eyes against the driving rain with an open hand, I could see that less than one hundred yards away was a gigantic round rock sticking out of the water. Close behind it was a beach that seemed to be sheltered from the breaking waves. Without hesitation, I steered my sluggish vessel toward the monolith, and with the skill born of panic, I managed to jibe the boat violently and scrape past this giant rock into a semiwaveless, semiwindless wilderness of boiling water. Without hesitation I rushed forward, cutting furiously with my unsheathed knife at every sheet and halyard on board, causing everything aloft to drop violently from the sky and onto the deck. Diving wildly and slicing the preventer holding my anchor onto the deck, I spun on my bottom side and kicked the anchor from its cradle to hear it splash soundly into the sea, followed closely by a symphony of clanging and banging chain being dragged up from its locker and through the fair-lead, falling into the water. I grabbed the chain-break on the anchor windless with both hands and pulled with all my might. There I sat, hopelessly blinded by the jib that had covered me up as it fell over the deck and into the water.

The exodus of ground-tackle stopped, and slowly but surely, my sinking boat began to turn toward the wind. There I could see, as luck turned me one more a favor, we were coming to rest merely a hundred feet from a large gravel-covered beach. As the anchor grabbed a tight hold and the bow stopped turning, I felt the ominous bump of keel meeting bottom, while *Nattily Ann* rose and fell in the gentle sheltered swell. I cleared the sail off me and slowly paid out as much chain as I could, in hopes *Nattily Ann* would come to rest close enough to this sheltered shore so that I could repair her bottom. Bumping the bottom then sliding forward and aft on the swell, *Nattily Ann* started to list, and then she stopped her backward motion, pulling up almost broadside to this sheltered beach. The gentle broken back swell was pushing her stern slowly into the bottom, but she could hold the sea out no longer, so there she was to stay.

Working my way back on the listing deck, I pulled my soaking sails out of the water and wrapped them around the boom as best I could. Folding and tucking the heavy wet canvas from the healing position of the deck, with lake water lapping at my feet, I now know that I was in shock. The enormity of what had just transpired was yet to settle in my mind. I tied the main gaff over the main boom and saw where that cracking sound had come from. The gaff had clearly started to break under the pressure of ferocious wind and pounding waves. Nervously fidgeting with the broken rigging and securing things that were out of place, I remember having the embarrassing feeling that someone might be watching me and judging me for my actions.

My intention was to attend to my boat, as I would have if she had been tied to a dock, but this was no dock. As I looked down into my hopelessly flooded cabin, I was struck softly on my neck and shoulder by a shaft of warming sunlight. I looked up to see that the storm had broken out on the lake, and what was left of it was swirling away, carrying along with it a noisy crew of lightning and thunder. Listening to thunder away in the distance was a fearsome relief after what I had endured only moments ago. The warming sun was pursuing the rain, and warmth was once again filling the air.

Time had lost all dimensions to me, and the memory of my ordeal was confused and blurry in my mind. All I knew was that I was here, safe on a beach in God knew where, with the love of my life settling down on the bottom of some lonely, isolated cove. Like a rock falling from the sky and landing on my head, the realization of my plight struck. I was shipwrecked! If only I could have sustained the fight a little longer, we might have avoided the bottom, but fate had dealt the hand, and it was already played. Anger and rage began to battle with self-loathing at that realization and punched me with a wicked blow. Why had I slept so soundly? In all my years at sea I had never let sleep captured me in such a way. My negligence had led me into this loathsome situation, and my ship was possibly lost forever! My self-hatred for this debacle would surely haunt me for a lifetime, however long I might have left. My mind fought to wake itself from this awful nightmare, but try as I did, there came no relief from the truth: I was hopelessly stranded, and at my own hand at that!

I slowly became aware of a stinging pain emanating from my right arm. I noticed there was blood on the deck and floating crimson in the fluid that now occupied most of my slanting cockpit. Pulling on my arm to check my elbow, I could see a gash about two inches long across it but, thankfully, not too deep a cut. Whatever had scraped across me had cut my rain gear open as well. This I could see as I retrieved my jacket before the sea carried it off with every other floating thing I owned. More than likely I had cut myself when I fell to the cabin floor while trying to start my motor, which was now encased in three feet of cold lake water.

A quick jump down into the flooded cabin to retrieve the first aid kit shocked me into the reality that, aside from the cold water, I now had nowhere to sleep. The water was hip deep, and pulling the kit from under the settee required submerging my arm to the shoulder in the cold, cold water. I was glad this was August water; I could not imagine what it would be like in November. Wrapping wet bandages around my leaking arm, I surveyed the beach, which I was so fortunately a guest of. Where my boat was slowly nesting was all a smooth round pebbly shore, but farther down the shore, I could see there was a level sandy expanse. For all I could see in my quick survey, there were no roads or pathways, but the beach at that point was wide and flat. That was where I would make my camp for now.

Suddenly time had no meaning to me. My trip was done, and my dream of a peaceful, rewarding sail was irrefutably altered. The reality was that I was here and had nowhere else to go. It took a while for my reluctant mind to accept this truth, and the truth was overwhelming; I was, by God, here to stay.

Fortunately, the shore was close enough to the stern of my boat to allow me to toss all the light salvage into a pile. The heavier stuff

I fastened with line and pulled ashore. The task of retrieving food supplies, bedding, and books took most of the remaining daylight. I toiled without stop until I was sure *Nattily Ann*'s belly was as empty as it could be for now. What a sad sight to see such a brilliant vessel lying so unceremoniously entombed, with her bow fully submerged and water slowly rolling over parts of her that were never intended to feel such a cold embrace. Later in my ordeal, I sketched a picture of her in that repose, and it hangs on my wall to this day as a constant reminder of that horrible experience.

4

BEFORE DARK I lit a fire, and aside from the possibility of it being seen from out on the lake where some curious soul might take a look, it was my warm companion on that first lonely night. I wrapped myself in what was left of my headsail to ward off the cool summer lake air. Every action, every movement, every scene was analyzed over and over, again and again in my mind. There was no strength left in me as I lay next to the fire and watched the last shafts of light from the same day I had seen begin. It was the end of a day I would never forget.

How could I have ever let this thing happen? Before sleep, I sat trying to bear the pain of making an honest entry into my log report of the accident. The glow of the fire gave an almost surreal vent for the words I so painfully scribed to the paper:

> 17:45 August 5. The end of this day finds *Nattily Ann* of Duxbury foundered on a lonely Canadian shore through nothing short of the negligence of her captain, Patrick Thomas Murphy. Rescue is uncertain and a search for help or an escape route will begin in the morning. Rescue or extraction is uncertain, so may God watch over my soul.

I slept restlessly that night, continually viewing my ordeal. Once, as the fire was spitting and dwindling just before dawn, I was overwhelmed with a phenomenal wave of loneliness. For a brief moment, there was a foreboding sense that no one would ever see or hear from me again. Bracing myself against a fear that felt like my world was entering into a weightless, confused blur of emotion, I rose from my canvas cocoon and forced myself into action, searching to find some sign of civilization in the predawn light. A search by torchlight found nothing in the way of a trail or even an animal path to the water. This little beach seemed to be untouched by humans or animals and possibly was accessible only by water.

I returned to my pile of possessions stacked haphazardly on the beach and opened the brass and cherrywood box that contained my sextant. Setting my handheld compass down on the closed box, I raised my sextant and took a fix as the planet Mars sat brilliantly sparkling on the southwestern horizon, and then I turned my instrument toward Polaris. I marked the calculations and proceeded to determine where it was that I had been made a castaway. As fate would have it, we had not made it to the Canadian shoreline. With the sun rising over the trees that first morning, the chart showed that the storm had put us on the western shore of a small island named Montreal, about eight long miles offshore from Canada's wilderness. I could not have gotten more off course if I had tried. My sleep and fate had guided me to this lonely little island on the cold shores of Lake Superior.

The chart, as rudimentary as it was, was not lying about where it was we had found ourselves. From where I sat, munching on a dry biscuit to keep the gnawing hunger at bay, I watched my hapless boat being washed by little waves she would have no part of if it were her choice. I needed an escape plan, but my mind had no thoughts that morning other than the stark realization of where I was now, and I was not in any way happy about it.

That morning, after the waves settled down, I launched my little eight-foot pram. My search of the shoreline showed no signs of life at all. In fact, I found this island to be quite inhospitable with nothing that resembled my newly found acre of land for shelter and an ample driftwood supply. My prayer to the Great Spirit had had some effect, it would seem, because the only spot that a boat could anchor and land a person on this island was right where I had landed. Otherwise, every inch of shore exposed to the lake was strewn with large jagged rock formations and unfriendly bluffs.

With the realization that it was the only spot we could have survived on, my spirits somewhat revived. Any other grounding would have surely meant my death. To worry about my boat when my life was so close to finished seemed trivial at that point, and the first breath taken at that realization was sweet indeed. Stepping from my pram to the shore of my new home felt like stepping on familiar ground. This was my new home.

Within a week's time, I managed to build a small fort right in the middle of what was now my sandy residence. Being handy with carpentry tools, and having a bountiful supply of driftwood, I managed to build a very useful wooden frame that I draped my mainsail over. With my jib sail for a floor, my new dwelling sprang to life. Cutting and sewing here and there, the tent looked as if it should have been in a military encampment. Its style was that of a walled tent that stood seven feet in the middle. About eight feet wide and ten feet long, there was plenty of room to move around on those wet, cold, or dreary days that drove a person inside. My ship's small iron cook stove was placed almost in the middle, and with the teapot steaming away, I'll be damned if the place didn't almost have the feel of a home.

Outside the front door flap, I pounded driftwood into the sand on end then lashed each piece to its neighbor in a way that looked similar to a stockade fence. Its purpose was to break the relentless wind that sometimes run up the beach and rattled my canvass walls all night through. I could sit leaning against the wall, looking out to the lake, and tend the ever-burning signal fire. Cooking food and watching for any vessel that might, by some stroke of luck, pass by, was my daily task, which became a routine.

I erected a tripod to hold my good-sized stew pot, which was made of heavy iron and did a wonderful job of spreading the heat evenly so as to not scorch the food. Mostly it held a mixture of canned meat, fish, or salt pork mixed with potatoes, dried beans, and canned tomatoes with lake water. I became quite adept at lifting the heavy-laden pot onto the hook above the flame using a forked stick. I designed an ingenious floating device that suspended a fish line with a hook and a small piece of salt pork. The line went from an anchored floating boat finder, through a pad eye on the float's bottom, and then to the beach where I rigged a spring-loaded rattrap with a stick and a piece of red cloth on the end. When the line was tugged, the trap would pop, and the flag would rise. All I had to do then was pull up a second line with the hook, fish, bait, and all right up on shore. Owing to the excellent taste of the pork, there were many fish pulled over those pebbles and into my stew pot.

As I look back, I realize those were fine days indeed. At that time I figured there would be some sort of vessel passing by, or possibly an aircraft, and I was prepared to toss a large tightly bound bundle of birch bark onto the fire that would cause billowing clouds of black smoke to erupt, hopefully bringing attention to my position. What I did not know was that any traffic that did venture by went past on the other side of the island, away from the open lake.

I found the place to be friendly, somewhat inviting, and full of surprises. Aside from a flock of noisy and curious seagulls, there was no sign of life except for some old ship's framing and planking that I found buried in the sand. There was nothing there to remind me of the existence of other humans anywhere on this planet. For all I knew, I might have been the last human living on the planet, owing to some great smallpox disaster of unfathomable proportions. Many hours on the island were spent entertaining this fantasy.

I often dreamed of what it would be like to live in an Indian village and survive by your own wits. Life for those early North Americans must have been hard and very primitive, but I am sure the simplicity of it allowed a long and full life. Could I imagine not even having a pot to cook in or a knife to cut my meat? They had neither soap nor store-bought clothing, for that matter. Everything they had they made themselves. Early European settlers would have fared much worse had it not been for the experience of the Indian population in those days. Many would have perished, and America might have had many fewer settlers without their help.

The nights stranded on that island were wondrous, and the sky was a splendid show. I found my many hours of sky watching to be a great joy. There was a never-ending spectacle of motion and color and streaks of light falling from the heavens into the flat reflective lake. Meteors and sparkling planets danced in an ever-changing ballet of light and motion. The northern lights display would light the sky as if the moon were in its fullest stage, colors of every imaginable hue lapping at the splendid northern celestial array. Lying on my back with my face to the sky, I would watch the sky endlessly, listening to the unique sounds that smooth round stones make when they roll over each other as the waves wash over them and then recede from their presence. It is one of the most pleasing sounds I have ever heard, and if I could bottle it and take it with me, it would always make my drift into slumber a much more pleasant journey.

Another interesting thing was the seagulls that spent their nights in a large flock a few short hundred feet from my camp. They were not bad neighbors except for the chatter they engaged in every time they returned to the beach to sleep for the night. There was incessant bickering and fighting for position in the flock before, miraculously, the noise would instantly stop, and they would all go to sleep. I was always fascinated that even though there would be no sign of a seabird anywhere around, as soon as I started to clean a fish, the whole clan would show up, seemingly out of nowhere.

There must have been twenty or thirty of these birds. They were not shy and seemed to have a well-established pecking order. One of the flock stood out above the others, however. He was the undisputed boss, and all gave him respect, which is true of any flock of birds, I would imagine, except that this bird had one outstanding handicap. The poor fellow possessed only one leg. I assumed he lost the other leg in some bird war or over a delicious scrap of carrion or something of the sort. Hopping around on that one limb, he would push and shove without ever losing his balance or poise. Steely eyed and impressive, one leg or not, he stood tall in that flock.

He would land upright in the middle of any disagreement over the fish guts, instantly hop to the offending tidbit, and consume it without one word of challenge from the others. In truth, I became quite fond of this fellow, as did he of me. As time passed, I was amazed by the gregariousness this fowl possessed. Rufus actually got used to standing on my knee as I sat at the fire and allowed me to feed him with my hand. I named him Rufus because he reminded me of an old one-legged salt I once knew by that name. Rufus would sit on my knee for hours after the rest of the flock had gone to sleep, and I swear he would listen contentedly to my rambling. It was nice to have something to talk to, and although the conversations were a little one-sided, they were always cordial. I thought about whittling up a little wooden leg for him, but after I had a good laugh over the thought of a bird with a wooden leg and a patch over his eye, I forgot about it.

That friendly bird began to spend less time with his flock and more time with me. He followed me, hopping around after me and occasionally jumping into flight when I walked too fast for him to keep up. It was somewhat like having a dog that was often underfoot. Old Rufus actually became somewhat of a pest and caused me to take stock of our friend/fowl relationship. Although he was overly attentive, I was sure it wasn't because I fed him scraps from time to time; I felt sure this bird actually liked me. Truth be known, I was very fond of him and missed him when he wasn't there. The thought of Rufus standing on his one appendage, bracing himself skillfully against a howling wind with feathers flapping wildly in the breeze, warms my heart to this day.

This island-bound, semi-euphoric time was short lived. I had made it all the way to the fifteenth of September without sighting one single boat. Not even a canoe had floated past. What is more, there was a period of three days during which the wind blew out of the north, and at one point the rain turned to snow and sleet. The fact that it could snow so early in the year startled me into the reality that I might be stuck here alone all winter with only my limited supplies. Even if I caught many fish every day, there wouldn't be enough dried fish to make it through the winter. The realization that I might not survive panicked me into action.

For three stormy days I stayed inside, venturing out only for necessities. I sat at my makeshift drawing board in the warm shelter of my tent and listened to the wind-driven rain pelting loudly at the world outside and drew up three plans. I will admit the feeling of being safe and warm inside made me wonder why I would ever consider going out on the lake again. The lake would build into a thunderous roaring froth and smash against anything that remained unsheltered from it. Such enormous power would have broken my boat to pieces if she were lying broadside to that fury.

During a bathroom break one day, I found Rufus standing steadily on his one little leg in the rain, looking soaked and cold. On my way back in, I scooped him up and took him inside with me. He looked pitifully rain soaked and dejected; I cradled him against my chest and stroked his little feathered head as we sat next to the warmth of my small cook stove. He was a large bird and solid under his beautiful white and gray feathers. His eyes glowed brightly as he turned his head from side to side to survey the new surroundings.

I felt I had no choice but to domesticate this poor fowl. Rufus instantly adapted to indoor living and found his spot squatting next to the flicker of the warming candle lantern on my salvaged ship's table. As I worked on my plans each evening, calculating and pondering, it was nice to have a companion to share my ideas with. I would sit with the bird cradled in my left arm, and as I gently rubbed my finger under his neck feathers, I could swear I heard him purr like a kitten. In truth, it was Rufus who ultimately gave me the method of my escape. There is no doubt in my mind that, had it not been for that bird, I would not be writing this narrative now.

Early on, I had contemplated escape by water, but a bitterly cold dive into the lake had shown that my boat had a broken back, and nothing I could do would patch the places where water could get in. The only way she would ever float again would to be lifted by a strong crane and carried on a barge to safety. My dinghy was too small and fragile for the task of rowing me and provisions the fifteen or twenty miles to an unknown shore, and a driftwood boat would never survive this lake.

My next plan was to wait until the lake froze over and walk to mainland Canada, which seemed to make sense, but I had no way of knowing if the lake would freeze solid, and falling through the ice would mean certain death, so that would be a last resort. Even if I dragged my dinghy, being alone in an unknown place in freezing conditions could surely turn fatal.

Despite all my planning, all the risks seemed too great, so I began preparing to stay for the winter. That would require building a permanent shelter and laying in supplies of fish and whatever else I could catch to eat. Firewood would be plentiful with the enormous supply of driftwood about, but stacking and cutting it into lengths would take considerable time. I could not help but think that these might be my last days on this earth if I did not work feverishly to survive.

I drew up a plan for a makeshift cabin, and I must admit, the prospect of building it excited me. Even so, I reluctantly I took on this project, for I knew my chances of survival over the long winter were minimal. Unfortunately, my other options were weak at best. The thought of somehow winching my vessel up to the beach for a winter shelter intrigued me, but that plan was put aside because of its size and its considerable weight. It was then that I began an earnest appeal to the Great Spirit to give me a way or to send help. Little did I know that help would come in the form of a one-legged seagull.

One day, as I was stacking wood next to the signal fire, I accidentally dropped a log on its end, and it almost landed right on top of Rufus. All I could do was watch as the six-foot log fell directly toward the bird's tiny body, but much to my delight, Rufus sprung up out from under that log just at the last moment with an agility and speed that saved his life. He didn't slow down either but kept flapping his wings until he had gained a safe altitude far over my head. I remember shouting up to him, "Rufus, you lucky bastard! I wish it could be that easy for me!" *Clang!* Like a single strike of the ship's bell, a thought went off in my head that would eventually turn into reality. I would fly out of this sandy prison. I would build an airplane and fly away like a bird! Rufus showed me the way to escape this place, and escape I would. Thank you, bird!

O NE OF THE benefits of my years of work was time and money to do things. As a result, I had studied flight and actually taken flying lessons, obtaining my aircraft operator's license, issued by the federal government. I had even had a turn at the helm of one of Mr. Ford's trimotor airplanes. It was a beautiful large bird with room for twelve persons on board. How amazed I became when I realized that something that big could actually leave the ground. What is more, while attempting to make my first practice landing in the thing, it seemed not to want to leave the air at all. It floated and floated more than I ever imagined it could. Those big spruce wings would have held the Empire State Building aloft for my money.

Like everything else I have done, I studied it thoroughly. Aeronautics became a hobby of mine, and I was now becoming obsessed with the idea of building a flying machine. Everything I knew about flight raced through my mind. I knew I had the tools and enough canvas in stock to put some crude airship together, but what to power it with still evaded me. My little ship's engine had enough power, but it was built out of cast iron, and I feared it weighed way too much to be useful. Aircraft engines of the day were mostly made from aluminum and cooled by the air that flowed past them.

This imaginary contraption would have to be small and light, with sufficient power to lift me and my survival goods far enough over the trees and across the water to somewhere on the mainland where civilization might exist. That would require a lighter engine than I had. Plus, if it could be built, where would I fly it from, and how far would it require to get it off the ground and above the trees?

There was a shortage of writing paper, so I drew plan after plan in my logbook. The wings would be easy. I could construct them from torn-up deck planking with canvas stretched over each wing and shrunk tight with painted shellac. A simple one-surfaced wing and a box-constructed fuselage would do, but I had doubts about my engine, which was safely stored beneath three feet of very cold water at the moment. I dreaded the task, but if there was any hope of using it, the engine had to be removed from my soaking vessel, so off I set to tackle the task. With pant legs rolled to the knees and wrenches in hand, I stood in crotch-deep water of a very uncomfortable temperature and unfastened every nut and bolt attaching the boat to the motor. Leaning over the almost totally submerged engine, I managed to free the transmission from the shaft by feel alone. The entire task took a day and a half, mainly due to numerous trips to the firepit to replenish the warmth to my limbs.

Using the main boom block and tackle, I fastened the motor and began to hoist it out of its cradle. My expectations were much diminished as I pulled the engine through the companionway. The weight of the engine turned out to be much more than I had thought. My rigging was under tremendous strain, and even though I had a three-to-one purchase on the blocks, the pulling was heavy. This engine, compared to a lighter airplane engine, would make the task of building a flying machine much harder. I thought that building much larger wings might be an answer, so back to the drawing board I went. With my Red Wing engine drained of all the fresh water it held and proper lubrication to restore it, I looked at it resting on the sand at the edge of the lake and wondered how it could possibly be coaxed into pulling me and my life off the ground and into the air. Fifteen horsepower just wasn't enough!

Wrestling with the thought of lifting off the ground in any way I could set my mind ablaze with ideas. I had seen photos of a German airship which was filled with a lighter-than-air gas then propelled through the air with two engines with propellers. I pondered and doodled, pondered and doodled, until I realized that in my doodling, I had drawn the outline of something that resembled a dirigible. I could very likely build a dirigible out of wood and canvas large enough to lift life and limb off this island.

Then I remembered that two Frenchmen, brothers named Montgolfier, had built a balloon-shaped object and filled it with hot air and lifted humans to a dazzling height back in the seventeen hundreds. I had plenty of canvas and lots of wood for fuel. That was it! I could build a balloon! Even an umbrella will lift into the sky if it is held and released over a hot fire. Not having any gasses at hand, a hot-air-filled bag would lift weight in proportion to its size. It was simple physics.

That wonderful idea took direction, and before long, I had several realistic drawings; all of which required air to be heated in sufficient amount to lift everything attached to it to an altitude of one hundred feet then rowed or paddled in a forward direction by manpower alone. This design eliminated the weight of my iron motor, some two hundred plus pounds, and if constructed light enough, I might be allowed to stay aloft for up to two hours or more.

I estimated that my supply of new unused tanbark canvas, plus the six bags of used sails, including my tent, would give enough volume to lift over two hundred and fifty pounds easily. I used a rough equation that is used to figure displacement of water in relation to a boat to approximate the dimensions-to-weight ratio, but I had no idea if it was correct or not.

This was definitely the way to go. The plan was set, and I was committed. I carefully began to build the contraption and resigned myself to take as long as necessary to do it right. It was a tremendous risk, I knew, but one I felt I was up to. The idea was to lift above the trees, drift effortlessly out over the water, and hopefully make it to the safety of the Canadian mainland. I felt the whole thing could be accomplished in about the same time it would take to build a cabin and gather supplies of food and wood for the winter. It was an all-the-eggs-in-one-basket kind of thing, but I felt sure about this plan.

Again I used my limited knowledge of mathematics to estimate temperature differentials and displacement. I was already aware of the best method for making charcoal for my fuel out of wood, and driftwood seemed to make excellent charcoal. There was already a good supply under the ashes of my fire pit, which had burned continuously for almost ten weeks. All I needed to do was to figure out how to extinguish the flames at the height of the blaze and retrieve the partially consumed wood after cooling.

The design began to gel, and drawings showed a cigar-shaped envelope with a light wooden frame holding the canvas bag on its top, with the bottom suspending my dinghy and myself, charcoal supply, and provisions on board. Once again I turned to Rufus for help. Stretching his wings out and making sketches, I found the way his wings hinged and folded made it possible for him to swim through the air, not much different than a turtle swims through the water. I would duplicate seagull wings and affix them to my pram so I could row through the air in much the same manner as I would row through the water.

It seemed to me this plan might just work, and all I needed to do was test my theory with a model. I constructed an almost-scale model out of paper sack, wire coat hanger, a jar lid, and some twine. It was large enough to hold one lantern candle on the jar lid for heat to cause a temperature differential and lift the whole mess skyward, which it did, right out into the lake. To my joy the paper and wire airship lifted off the sand and soared to a height of about twenty feet. There it met a draft and sailed out over the lake, where it promptly caught a downdraft and crashed into the water with a sizzling thunk! Crash it did, but fly it did also!

I was convinced this was my salvation. There would be an airship as yet unknown to man plying the wilderness sky somewhere in North America, and I would be the only living soul aware of its existence. If this plan actually worked, it would be worthy of note. On the other hand, if I failed, there would be no knowledge of my escape attempt or efforts to be found. I would be lost at sea or perish in the great forests of Canada, but this was a chance I was willing to take. One thing was sure, I had enough canvas and wood to do the job.

For three days in a row, I unfastened planking from *Nattily Ann*'s deck, carefully splitting some of the planks into long pieces about one inch wide by drawing a knife blade from one end to the other. To my delight, all but a few of the fir planks accommodated me in this effort, and I ended up with fine stock for construction of my new craft.

I started from the dinghy up and built a crude driftwood frame to hold the balloon off the ground, well above where the dinghy and firepot would hang. The firepot was to be my four-gallon iron cooking kettle full of charcoal suspended just below the canvas bag where I sewed a round opening using a metal ring made from the ship's bronze rub-rail onto what was an otherwise completely enclosed potato-shaped bag. Work on this project went well, and within a couple of days, the support frame and the balloon frame were up. I lashed the bag frame with light line and, with a bountiful supply of thread from my sewing kit, sewed leather grommets on the canvas where it would attach to the outside framing.

By the end of the first week, half the bag was sewn, and the other half was cut and well on the way. Even though my hands became cracked and sore from the constant threading and pulling the needle through the canvas, progress was swift, but I feared that the process of making the charcoal would be long and difficult. With more and more signs of winter flying south overhead and snow popping out of swift-moving clouds, I began to hurry even more.

My first attempt at securing fuel was to relocate the fire. That was easy enough, but the absence of a good shovel made the task more difficult. The bulk of the fire was coerced from its origin with long sticks I used to shove and sweep the fire to its new location a mere four feet away. After the original fire was put out, I picked through it and placed the best chunks of charred wood inside a large sail bag. I calculated that there was room and weight allowance for two of these bags in the dinghy with provisions and myself.

The rest of the charcoal was made by painstakingly stacking wood in a pile that would allow the fire to grow evenly, and after the entire pile was fully engulfed, I frantically tossed water over the pyre and smothered the flames. I soon found that small fires were easiest to handle in this effort. I would build several fires at a time and then scurry back and forth to the water's edge to fill my two canvas buckets and trudge up the loose gravel embankment to douse the fires.

This exercise took more than a day due to the energy my fifty-four-year-old body lacked. I had only enough energy to build and extinguish six fires at a time, so a good night's rest was necessary between sessions. Each fire yielded only five to six pounds of charcoal, and I would need a total of about one hundred pounds to safely stay aloft, if indeed I could get aloft.

With luck, I would affect the original lift from wood on the ground, and after enough heat had filled the bag and it was tugging on its restraints, I would cut the tether and be lifted with the two bags of charcoal, whereby the use of this fuel would lighten the load as I went along. At that time, I had no idea of how much fuel it would take or whether I could even get the fire hot enough to cause the bag to fill with hot air at all. One thing I did know was that there needed to be enough cold air in the bag to be displaced by the hot air I hoped to generate with my charcoal. This would require the bag to be partially suspended and somewhat full of air to begin with. I accomplished this by inserting one long deck plank straight up from the opening in the bottom and stretching the bag up in a tentlike configuration. Then, midway to each end of the bag, I inserted a bow-like structure made of thin spruce planking that held the bag aloft so it would fill easier with the hot air.

Finally the craft was taking shape, and fitting the dingy to the main frame was a sign of things to come. Fastening it fore and aft would keep it relatively in place, and hanging straight down under the bag would support the weight of coal, booty, and me. I screwed a seat back to the thwart bench on the dinghy so I could rest my back while rowing. The wings of canvas were almost done. All that was left was to cut my oars short and fasten them to the first section of wing, which I had fashioned to emulate the folding wing of a seagull. Rufus watched me closely, as if he were the supervisor. Balancing one-legged on a log, suspiciously swinging his head from side to side, he showed no signs of fear as the large wings flapped open with a loud crack.

My theory was that as I pushed the oar handle aft toward the back of the dinghy, it would cause the wings to fold in two on the hinges as they went forward, behind my back. The wings would then crack open when I pulled the oar handles toward me, making the wings catch the air and pop open, using wind resistance to propel me along in a forward direction. The direction would be controlled by a vertical fin, which I attached to a long pole on the back of the rig, thus stabilizing my efforts.

The theory was sound, but the application proved to be quite a different story. Upon finishing my first "air oar," I found that pulling the oar back toward my chest caused an uncontrolled wrenching effect that twisted the oar handle right out of my hand. This problem I eliminated by taking the oarlock out and replacing it with large iron keel bolt placed through the center of the oar handle where the oarlock would have been. Drilling the hole in the wooden oar shaft would weaken the oar, true, but at the time it seemed the only solution, and it did work.

Sitting in the dingy, which was resting on the sand, with my back to the bow, I tried the wing, and much to my surprise, the light canvas wing unfolded and caught the air with such force that it began to swing the little dingy around on its axis. I was somewhat worried that the weight and resistance of the wings might tire me faster than rowing through water and wondered if the forward motion of the vessel would be maintained if I needed to rest between strokes. I knew that a well-designed boat will lose little speed while the oars are lifted out of the water, but what resistance this craft would have to the air I did not know.

On the sixteenth night of construction, I sat huddled next to my signal fire and looked cautiously at my amazing hermaphrodite flying rig. Had anything ever been built to resemble this craft? A craft it was, with the forward and aft portions being narrower than the middle part, and from the look of it, the bag was proportionately large enough to hold sufficient hot air to cause the lift I would need to seek freedom. I was pleased with my efforts, and all that was left to do was build an experimental fire in the pot and see what happened. I had fashioned a beautiful big bag that looked as foreign and different as anything I had ever seen. There was a sense of pride at this accomplishment, but would it fly?

The fire was lit in the predawn hours, when the air was coldest and stillest. Charcoal was thrown in the pot and ignited with the help of a cup of gasoline fetched from the ship's supply. A great flame erupted, and a fear of burning the thread holding the ring in place overwhelmed me. After the flame subsided, I could see the fire's lapping at the canvas and thread did no harm. It might be a different matter after the ring had been heated for an hour or so. This problem I settled by wrapping asbestos cloth from *Nattily Ann*'s exhaust pipe and seizing it with wire to the ring, thus retarding any effect the flame and heat may have.

To my delighted surprise, the bag began to fill with hot air. I was startled from my wondrous observations by the clatter as the plank holding the canvas aloft was freed from its task, dipping its end into the pot, dispersing sparks and hot coals all over the place. It was going to work! Now the only thing would be its ability to lift me from my prison-ground and propel me long enough to find civilization.

That night in my restless sleep, I was visited by dreams of failure. Startling visions of the model falling out of the sky into the cold waters of Lake Superior repeated themselves. I lay there staring skyward with thought after thought of what I might expect to happen in this endeavor. As the night wore on, fear was replaced by solid resolution to see this thing through. It was literally do or die. My one-legged feathered friend must have sensed my fear, for he stayed outside my tent and made a racket until I brought him to the shelter of my home, which quieted him at once. It is amazing how much comfort such a frail bird could give to a human.

The day came when I knew that I could wait no longer; I was as ready as I could be. I would take only the bare necessities. My rigging knife and the ship's pistol, a .45-caliber Colt Navy model revolver, would be a must. There would be a need for my wool coat, warm clothing, and a bedroll. Food would consist of hard biscuits, dried beans, beef, and fish; with a canteen full of the lake water for my thirst; one small cooking pot; and my last bag of coffee beans. A handheld compass, my pocket watch, and a lantern powered by batteries would aid me in navigating. Aside from the logbook, my knife and a pocket notebook with my name and address etched on the leather cover, there was little else weight restrictions would allow. With supplies, fuel, and me, I figured the package, dinghy and all, weighed just less than three hundred pounds. It was more than I wanted to carry, but there was nothing in the lot I could do without.

I rigged an anchor and line so that, if there was sufficient lift to gather vertical speed, I could let go of the anchor line, which I would be holding closely in case something went wrong in the crucial initial moments. There was two hundred feet of line, which I felt would help me control the assent until I was well above the rocks and trees. If the need arose, I could pull on the line and return to the launch site unharmed, in theory.

As dawn broke on my last day on that beach, I sat, looking longingly at my beautiful sunken boat. She was a wreck and looked the part. Even though her beauty was evident above the situation, water lazily rolled over her semi-plank-less foredeck and lapped at the cabin windows. Memories of our times together swelled in my throat and eyes. Seeing something I trusted so unconditionally abandoned in this way was heartbreaking. Loneliness and longing to be with my wife filled my heart with emotion. Once again the combination of emotions left me dizzy with the feeling of falling through some hole in the earth or sky, weightless and alone, leaving the feeling that maybe I did not exist at all.

Fortunately, Rufus seemed to be aware of my depression and hounded me mercilessly, screeching loudly and persistently for me to feed him and pay attention to him. His helplessness dragged me from the self-pity I had somehow let in like an uninvited visitor. Having domesticated a bird in this manner seemed quite amusing to me, and the arrogance this creature exhibited made me happy. Rufus was a true character and his company had been invaluable to me in the time I had spent on this lonely beach. I would miss him dearly.

The dinghy was loaded and soundly fastened to the balloon. The wire cables holding the fire pot were checked and rechecked. The expansion stick was in place, and I was fully dressed in wool to guard against the cold. I folded a sheet of canvas onto the seat to ease seat discomfort and be used for shelter if needed. I was ready, but once again, as fate would have it, Mother Nature was not. She had decided to get restless, and the sky had suddenly become full of menacing clouds on departure morning. Snow spewed from fast-moving scud, and the wind became unyielding. My log reveals there was three days of this mess with me holed up in my considerably smaller bough-covered shelter, shivering against the cold.

Finally, on the twenty-ninth of October, the sky was clear and cold with no wind. I made an entry in my log stating my intentions. I blew out the lantern and exited what was left of my warm and friendly tent. The glow of the signal fire bouncing in reflection off my airship was almost dreamlike. Orange glowing canvas and wood with a little dinghy hanging, motionless beneath it, gave an image of awesome proportions. I could hardly believe that I had actually built this thing, and a thing of beauty it was. Never had I seen anything like it, and more than likely, it would never be seen by any human eyes beside mine. More is the shame!

I stoked up a fire in the pot, and as with my last try, flames leaped out at my balloon but caused no damage. Minutes went by like hours, and before thirty minutes were gone, the bag was noticeably starting to fill. First slowly, then rapidly, the thing took form. It was the first time I had seen how large the canvas bag really was, and its size was impressive. I fed the fire while standing next to the dinghy, and as I tested the rigging, I noticed a lightness developing. She was lifting under her own power and would be ready to fly at any moment.

Every minute or so I would look over my shoulder, hoping for a glimpse of the sun rising up through the trees to the east. I had started too early, and my supply of charcoal on the ground was dwindling rapidly. I would have to lift off before the sun was up and take my chances in the diminished light. Then, there before my eyes, the craft began to lift and tug on the anchor line, causing the cradle to become unstable, which was now only being held together by the resistance of the anchor line and the weight of the craft. I managed to remove the center strut using a long stick before it could catch on fire and ruin all my plans. Without thinking, I grabbed the hot strut by its smoldering end and instantly burned my hand. It was a foolish move, which would later come to haunt me.

It was time! Once again I turned toward the east to look for the sun as I stepped over the dinghy gunwale and sat down on the seat that I hoped would be my home until rescue, or at least freedom, was at hand. Unfortunately it was not to be! As I stepped into the craft, it sank down hard onto the ground, and all buoyancy was lost. How could this be? If this wasn't enough heat, it would be almost impossible to generate more. My weight calculations were obviously flawed, and something had to be jettisoned.

Then I remembered the small red metal can of gasoline I had left on the ground next to my tools. I jumped out and grabbed the can of gas and a blue porcelain drinking cup, which I promptly poured a small amount of gas into. I unloaded a little over half of one charcoal bag onto the dinghy floor and threw the rest on the ground to reduce the dinghy's weight. With a shot of gas, the fire jumped to life with a whoosh, and this time when I stepped in the dingy, it did not sink all the way down. I carefully reached over and poured another small amount of gas into the fire pot. The fuel sizzled for a moment then erupted in a burst of flame. Another shot of gas and the fire was roaring almost out of control. That was enough to make the anchor line go tight again.

First there was almost no movement, but as the seconds passed, I felt the tug of gravity and watched in wonder as the anchor line pulled gently through my hands. I was elated to find that the craft had a steady feel as the cradle crumbled and fell away, and the craft rose steadily and in no way seemed unbalanced. I must have lifted ten or fifteen feet before I noticed that I was lifting up to meet the sun on the other side of the island. What exhilarating joy I felt to be hoisted from the ground and watch my tent and fire and things I had become so familiar with becoming small beneath me. Here was a new sensation, like nothing I had ever felt before. Silently rising off the ground like that took my breath away and gave me a weird sensation in my stomach.

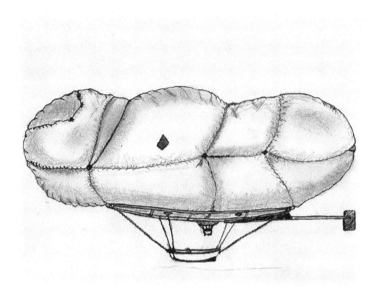

There I was, suspended under a large canvas bag full of very hot air, soaring to a dizzying height, when I realized that I was drifting slowly toward the west and out over the lake. Before I could hitch the anchor line and untie the oars, I had drifted past the beach, and there beneath me was a full view of my stricken boat bathed in an opaque, dark blue tomb, looking as abandoned as anything I had ever seen.

I quickly deployed the canvas wings and just as quickly began rowing. Two or three strokes then look down. Three more strokes then look. Six more strokes and then there was noticeable movement. I was moving forward, but I had stopped ascending. I could feel the craft starting to descend. One more shot of gas, and things were steady. A handful of charcoal was thrown onto the pier, and then I set about rowing. It became evident that rowing would move the craft, and I could easily control the direction by using unequal pressure on the oars, but I had to be steady, and attending the fire would have to be done rapidly or I would lose what momentum I had gained. Quickly I realized that this was to be no easy effort.

Another look down showed me to be about treetop level and climbing, so I decided to jettison the one tie I had with earth, other than gravity of course, and with a twist, the anchor line was gone, and there I was, off on a brand-new adventure. A quick shot of gas for good luck and a glance over my shoulder showed me I would probably clear the trees, and clear the trees I did. As the sun met my face, I found myself rowing over the forest that had encircled my existence for quite a considerable time, passing a mere ten feet below me.

I was so busy that I hadn't noticed the clamor ringing all around me. My flock of gulls was circling and screeching out early morning songs of farewell. I strained my neck looking for Rufus and finally saw him trailing behind, rising and falling to slow himself to meet my speed. I looked into his bright yellow eyes, and a pang of regret that I had not personally spent the time or energy to say goodbye to him tore through me. I may sound like a fool, but that bird meant very much to this man of the sea. That scruffy one-legged bird had challenged my despair and had shown himself to be its worthy opponent. From my lips, the words "Goodbye, old friend" were slowly spoken. Twisting one eye toward me, I thought I saw true sorrow from that bird. Could it be possible he knew we would never meet again?

6

THINGS SEEMED TO be going well. The birds had left me, with Rufus being the last to peel away, as I passed over the east end of my island. I felt for a while that he would follow me all the way to the Canadian shore, but as we approached Manitou Island's eastern shore, he became somewhat excited, as if he wanted me to return to our beach. He would turn away and then come back squawking loudly. Then he went away for good. In my years at sea I have had the company of many a character, but for some reason, this little feathered guy stuck to me like none before. It was common for me to set sail and leave friends behind, but this one was hard. I would always wonder about little Rufus as my days went on.

I had settled into a routine and was seeing the mainland of Canada just six or so miles ahead of me. Pulling on oars became somewhat automatic after I got the rhythm. It was but a short time before I had to wrap my hand with my handkerchief to ward off the pain from friction on the area I had burned earlier that morning. I took a short inventory of the coal, which I was using at the rate of about one pound every ten minutes. As I would take a handful of coal and throw it into the pot, I noticed that my hands were very black, and the washing I had given myself in the predawn dark had been for nothing. I could only imagine what the rest of me looked like.

I could feel the heat of the sun on my back, and my neck and ears received its soothing radiation. Without looking forward, which would interrupt my cadence, I watched Montreal Island grow smaller and smaller as the seconds turned to minutes. I noticed that the feeling of urgency had left my consciousness, and thoughts of home and Emma standing with me on our dock, watching the sea wash time away with every wave, filled my thoughts. Longing for home was foreign to me, but the lust for that security filled my mind with visions of everything from snowy winter mornings sitting next to my fire, to the garden that Emma tended so faithfully in the summer. Home is where I wanted to be, and even though we were less than a thousand miles apart, I felt I was as far away from Emma as I had ever been. I had traveled almost every point of the globe, but for some reason, I had never felt so far from home as I did at that very moment.

Secure in the hope that I had conquered this challenge and was within reach of the mainland, I began to relax. Once I had made the Canadian shore, all I had to do was to rise to a height that would give me a clear view of the country and find a road or farm or, if my prayer had been answered, a town. The view from two hundred feet above the surface would be unbelievable. If I could gain another three hundred feet, I was sure I would see Whitefish Point.

Glancing down at what had been glass-calm water below, I was startled to see waves forming. They were making a motion toward where I had just come from, and that was when I realized that I was closer to the island than when I last looked. I was losing ground! Lost in my thoughts, I hadn't noticed the increase in wind pressure on my neck, but now I was quite aware of it. A quick survey told the story. Even though I was halfway to land, the wind had risen, and my rowing had already been too little to counter it. It was that knowledge that set me into double-time. I strained at the oars until I felt there was progress being made, but every time I stopped rowing to fill the pot, the wind would want to swing the craft to one side or another and carry it away. Again I increased my efforts. My shoulders started to burn, and my arms ached with a pain like I had never known, and the wind was still rising. If I quit now, it would be the end of me, and my dreams of home would be dispersed with the wind like leaves off a dying tree. I held my breath and pulled five hard strokes at a time, then five more, like a swimmer grasping for air and distance. The fire would have to wait, and my hope was to get close enough to the shore to swim if I were to crash.

I prayed once again, but this time with real urgency. There was no question as to my fate if I failed now. What I needed was a break in the wind, if only for a moment, so I could rest and regain some of the strength in my back, which felt broken, shaky, and useless. What's more, the hanky had twisted off my hand, and the pain was excruciating as I was forced to row without its cushion. A fistful of charcoal went into the red-hot fire as fast as I could toss it there. I quickly rubbed some charcoal dust over my wounded hand and washed with it, like soap, for lubrication against the chafing that was starting to build a brutal fire between my hand and the oak oar handle. Filthy black-dust-filled sweat dripped off my nose and stung my eyes as I strained to keep my composure. My resolve to reach the shore was as strong as any as I had ever experienced. I would surely perish if this wind blew me out into the open lake. I was immersed in a tunnel of life that flowed away from me and then toward me in an alternate succession of pain and perverse pleasure mixed into a composition of raw survival.

I was alive and fighting for my very life. Alive as ever I had been was I there and then! Life was measured in moments and effort and nothing more! How much did I want to live and what would I give to keep my life? Pulling on those searing-hot oars, knowing that perishing in freezing-cold water was the alternative gave me a strength that came from well beyond my own abilities. Rowing directly into the wind was my only option, and that had taken me more to the south, where the distance to land increased considerably. The unbearable pain began to feel like one large searing orb surrounding my entire existence in that tiny little boat. All I was aware of was the sound of the canvas and fur wood wings cracking open with every excruciating stroke. What would give out first, a wing, an oarlock, my body? All sound and feeling seemed to come from the same source, and with every effort I made, they became stronger, and I became weaker. Time was running out!

Suddenly I became aware of a different sound. It was a loud scratching sound. Then I felt a bump, which startled me and forced me to turn around to see what it was. I was barely thirty feet off the water and had run into a tree! I had made it to the mainland, and there I had become tangled in a large oak tree! Without thinking, I dropped the oars and grabbed at a branch. I managed to get hold of one and held it tightly as the wind tried to swing my vessel away. Kicking off a boot, I managed to stretch out and pick up a coil of line with my toes from under the stern seat, and within moments, I had managed to tie my airship into the top of a large Canadian oak tree. As I did so, I could see that I was beginning to sink. Quickly I poured gas on the pyre, which exploded into a ball of flame and heat, once again lifting the ship up.

What a sight that must have been. Here was a strange craft, now hovering forty feet in the air, tied to a big oak tree. At least I was sheltered from the wind, and I quickly found that I could sit there and regain my strength while feeding the fire just enough to stay aloft. Drinking from my canteen and pouring fresh water over my head refreshed me enormously. My plan was to rest, and then, when I had half an hour of fuel left, I would go for it. I would lift and row as fast and hard as possible and hope to find some sign of human activity before running out of fuel and, thus, out of time. Even a river or stream would surely lead me to civilization.

I had used less fuel than estimated, thanks to the gasoline, which was still in plentiful supply. I poured the contents of the second charcoal bag onto the floor for easier access and closed my eyes for a moment. Strength reentered my aching body faster than it had left, but the pain was still there. My burned hand had started oozing some liquid other than blood, which mixed with coal dust to form a crusty black mess. I rewrapped my wounded hand with renewed hope for the best then sat there in a near stupor, resting as much as I could.

The smell of the forest gave me a new and welcome relief. All I really had to do was somehow jump into that tree and climb down then walk to civilization. I was finally free, but where was civilization? The green and mossy odor of the forest made me realize that the cursed wind had actually gone away. There was stillness in the fall-tinted treetops, and the water had once again become calm. I cast off from that lifesaving tree and doused the fire with a cup of gas all in one movement. Sinking at first then rising slowly above the tree, I could see a vast forest laid out below me like a great green and fall-colored carpet. Here and there temples of timber stuck out of the orange, red, and green sealike monuments or guideposts, relaying some ancient secret message. Without looking at my pocket compass, I just began to row inland and feed the fire. Putting distance between the lake and me seemed to be a good idea. In contrast to my previous row, this was an almost pleasant paddle into the country. Even my speed seemed to increase with every stroke. Every sixth stroke I would drop a chunk of coal onto the flames, and on several occasions, there would be the introduction of the slightest bit of gasoline. Within twenty minutes, I was cruising along at about one hundred feet above the trees with what seemed like motionless speed. I found that I could pause and survey the area without incident. I searched for signs of life at regular intervals until I began to wonder about the fuel situation.

Worry again entered the picture, for there were no clearings that I could drop into and nothing that resembled human intrusion anywhere in my view, and the fuel supply was running low. In every direction, all I could see was a vast forest. I had never seen such a thing. There, spread out below me was forest and more forest. The sight of the fall Canadian forest was nothing less than spectacular, and I felt quite grateful to be there and see it, in spite of the circumstances. I unrolled my chart and checked the compass. By my best guess, the nearest settlement might have been around thirty miles due south, but I hoped there was a farm or two with wide-open fields around these parts. My legs were beginning to cramp, but there was no room to stand and stretch while looking around. I had been in this small pram for almost two hours, and it was getting smaller by the minute.

Then, straight to the east, I caught a glimpse of something that looked like smoke rising up from the forest. It was only a glimpse, but that was enough to cause me to change course and pull hardily on the oars once again. I stuck to a compass barring and rowed like crazy, but when I turned around to look again, there was nothing but endless forest. I kept up the pace for another few minutes then ceased action to take another look. Still there was no smoke. As the airship slowed almost to a stop, and what was dangerously close to the last few chunks of coal were thrown on the blaze, I saw nothing. Quietly and slowly I pivoted in a complete circle until I had looked the entire area over several times with no sign of anything unusual. I was slumped in my seat, on the edge of despair, when I was startled to hear the sound of human laughter. Was this an apparition like the smoke, or did I really hear laughing? Every fiber of my being strained to hear it again, but nothing came. Then suddenly an eruption of laughter came up at me from directly beneath my perch!

Grabbing the gunwale and sinking into the bottom of my dinghy, I peered over the side. There, directly beneath me, were three men squatting around a small fire, sipping cups of what I figured must have been coffee. At almost the same moment, I smelled the smoke from their fire mingled with the faint smell of coffee. I was not dreaming! These were real humans! I was so startled by the discovery that I lost my voice as I began to give a hollow shout. My mouth was wide open, and my lungs had pushed air out over my dried lips, but nothing exited in the way of a sound. I was so happy to see humans I was out of control.

"Hello there!" I finally heard myself shout.

"Ahoy!" was the next word to drop from the sky.

The three men stopped their chatter, and one stood up, alertly looking around in every direction to see where the sound had come from.

"You there. I could use some help!" I squeaked.

All three of the men were standing now, jerking their heads from side to side, looking all around. Then one responded to my next call, looking straight up to see this strange contraption with a human head sticking out of it, drifting strangely above the treetops. His shock was so much that he lost balance and fell on his back, spilling coffee all over himself, never once taking his eyes off me. Lying there on his back with his two companions staring down at him, wondering what the heck was wrong with him, he pointed skyward with his empty cup and said, "Regard!" His companions looked up, and their surprise sent them reeling to the ground as well, tripping over each other in what looked to me to be a circus comedy routine. I laughed out loud and laughed again. There below me were three humans, and they showed no sign of being lost. They were healthy and happy and had coffee as well. Without thinking, I reached in my sack and retrieved my stash of coffee beans, which I promptly dropped overboard as an act of good faith. As I looked in my sack for more gifts to jettison, I became aware of the fact that I was sinking into the trees.

I remember sitting, dumbfounded, with my hand in my satchel, watching as the green, red, yellow, and orange sea swallowed me like some carnival ride and sent me bouncing straight to within five feet of the ground, where I jerked to a stop with my canvas air bag caught up in the forest's giant branches. I cannot imagine what these gentlemen were thinking at that time, but I will never forget the looks on their faces. Here was a strange-looking man, dressed in ragtag seaman's clothing, dropping down from the sky without warning, sitting there in a small boat suspended from a canvas bag, with an incredibly fierce smile stretching from one edge of his face to the other. I lifted my hand in a feeble wave.

"Hello" was all I could say.

"Bonjour!" was their somewhat questioning answer in unison.

I had not even climbed out of the dinghy when they hit me with a barrage of words spoken in what I assumed was French. These men were dressed in what looked like buckskin with colorful cloth sashes tied around their waists. Their stocking hats were ornate, with beautiful feathers sticking from each one, and they each had a bright-colored blanket-like coat with three red, yellow, and green stripes wrapping around the chest, but each in a different pattern. There was no doubt that these were descendants of the voyagers of old. I assumed they were hunters because they had three rifles leaning together in teepee fashion next to their coffee fire.

"Je ne parle pas François" was all I could muster. I do not speak French.

"Monsieur, I am Maurice. I speak *un peu Anglais*. Where are you from?" the tall one spoke to me.

"I have been shipwrecked on Montreal Island and have just escaped," I said, pointing toward the direction from whence I had just come.

"But what is this thing?" he said with a strong French accent as he swept his hand over the scene.

"I built this airship to carry me here, and I have found you, and I hope you will take me to Sault Ste. Marie."

"An airship?" He surprisingly laughed.

He turned to his friends and explained in French what I had said, his hands flying in every direction. His companions' faces went blank for a second while they digested the fact that I had actually flown over the water from a remote island and crashed into their presence right here in the tall wood.

"But what is your power, I see no motor?" The puzzlement in his face amused me as he looked all around the craft.

"I rowed here using these wings I built," I replied, pointing to the port side wing, which was hanging limply over the side.

The look on his face was that of wonderment as he tried to digest what it was that I had just told him. He turned once again to his companions and started a barrage of French that took many quick gestures. Then they all began to guffaw and slap their knees in the glee that something so bizarre should happen to them. Their laughter infected me, and for the first time in a long time, I found myself immersed in uproarious laughter right along with these fellows. What a wonderful feeling it was.

The trio inspected my craft and assisted me as I pulled it from its perch in the trees, sizing it up and actually touching various parts as if to convince themselves that what they saw was real. A few sentences were spoken between them, and Maurice turned to me and said, "Monsieur, this is my cousin John Paul and our good friend Frederic. We have the ability to take you to the rail tracks, where we will stop the train to Sault Ste. Marie. It passes to the south only once a day, and it is but fourteen or so miles from here. Although it will be impossible to tell you how long it might take us to do so. You see, we must hunt on the way there, for the railway carries our goods, and that may take some time. It is our livelihood, and it must be done. But what of your airship?"

What was an extra day or two? I thought. After all this time, what would a few extra days mean to me? I gratefully explained that if they took me to the rail line, they could have my precious airship, which sent them into songs of joy. They meticulously folded, tied it, and left it under a tree that they tied a red ribbon to so they could find it later. I was surprised how small the whole package was when they had finished folding and stacking the wooden parts neatly tied to the canvas. Amazingly, the entire deal fit into the dinghy, leaving room for nothing more.

T HESE GENTLEMEN OF the woods were very interesting to me. With few words, they gathered up their gear and led me down a narrow path that was identified only by a meandering line of bare dirt and sand wandering through a green and brown mixed leaf-covered forest floor. They swiftly navigated what must have been familiar territory to them but certainly not to me. There was a no-nonsense air about their movement. I was quite unprepared to follow these men in the manner in which they were obviously used to traversing the woods. I followed clumsily along several lengths back due to the shortness of my breath and fatigue in my legs, I suppose, and keeping up required much concentration. After about a mile or so of nearly running, I was forced to request a rest, citing leg cramping brought on by my extended lack of leg movement while sitting in my aircraft, which was somewhat true. I could tell they were slightly perturbed at this interruption but politely tried to hide it. I could only assume they were on some kind of timetable or deadline owing to the incredible speed of their gait. They showed no sign of exhaustion or heavy breathing after an excruciating hour of fast marching and stood silently as I sat on the ground, rubbing my feet after removing what I previously considered to be comfortable boots.

John Paul was kind enough to offer me a small canvas pack to sling over my shoulders, which made the task of carrying my goods much easier. I watched him pull it from under his orange, purple, and red knit waistband, showing me a lightweight cloth sack that, when full of my possessions, surprised me by its utility. It had two leather straps with adjustable buckles sewn on it, and after putting my arms through the two straps, it fit quite comfortably on my back.

These new companions struck me as confident in their movements. They were surely trying to figure what type of person I might be. I could only imagine how weird it must have been for them to have some strange man literally fall into their world and suddenly become a ward of theirs and surely a disruption to their usual routine. My initial impression was that they might have all been in their early to middle thirties and appeared as healthy as any males I had ever seen. Their stature reminded me of the tall African tribesmen I had seen pictured in the *National Geographic* magazines. There were uncomfortably few words spoken though and usually only in response to my questions. At any rate, I was in their care and would do my best to keep up. My rest may have been no more than ten minutes, but to them it must have seemed forever. Later I would come to know that these men traveled great distances on their hunting expeditions. Traversing ten miles in one hike was not foreign to them. Stopping to eat and rest sometimes only twice each day, they had found the human leg to be very useful in transporting a man with a heavy load over long distances with great efficiency.

Slipping my boots back on, tucking my pants into my socks and generally preparing myself for the continuing march, I began to notice my own incessant chatter echoing throughout the surroundings. I was the only one who had spoken more than two words the whole time we were there. Then I became aware that the trio was not paying any attention to me at all but was studying the all-encompassing forest, standing erect and at attention, in search of some errant noise or unseen movement that had caught their attention. I stood up and asked Frederic what they were looking for, but before I could finish my query, he reached out and placed his fingers up against my mouth. Without taking his gaze away from the woods to look at me, but before his hand was extracted from my lips, Maurice, in one quick motion, lifted his rifle to one open eye and pealed off a shot, the sound of which sent me jumping inches off the ground.

John Paul shouted something in French, and without hesitation, the three bounded off into the woods, side by side, in pursuit of what I did not know. The sounds of the shot and John Paul's words were still echoing through the trees as I watched these men spring into action and race away from me at an unnatural pace. The hunters ran like the wild beasts, lifting themselves effortlessly off the forest surface to bound over fallen trees and scrub brush with nothing to be heard but the swish of their legs scraping past twigs and branches. I watched as they ran rapidly out of sight over the top of a moss-covered knoll, skillfully steadying themselves with their buckskin scabbard rifles stretched out to their sides to act as balancing wands as the ground passed beneath them at an amazing speed.

Suddenly I realized that they might not be coming back to me, and I had better join the pursuit and quickly. I followed in their direction as best I could. It was but a short time before I realized everything in that forest looked pretty much the same. I stopped and listened in hopes of hearing some shouts or gunfire, but nothing came, so I continued in the direction I felt was correct. Confusion was setting in because there was not a single path or sign of their presence. No trampled brush or broken twigs were to be found. Nothing looked familiar. I dug my compass out of the pack and resolved to follow a compass course for a time, and if my companions were not found, I would surely find my way back to the beaten path, and then follow that path out to whatever was at its end.

Navigating those thick, heavy woods was not easy. Logs the boys had easily hurtled over sent me rolling over and falling off more than once. There were many ancient pine monsters lying across my intended path, and the time it took me to travel the distance they had gone certainly would have been twice or more what they had done. At their speed, they could have been a mile or more ahead of me by that point. Dying ferns were waist high, and a myriad of dried flowers and some mushrooms that had escaped the frost and all sorts of flora tended to drag my concentration toward sightseeing. It was well into fall but this forest showed little evidence of dying. Then one lonely protruding root reached up and caught my foot to send me careening, nose first, onto the soft mossy carpet. The sudden breath-expelling fall notwithstanding, I found the ground to be a very comfortable birth. I lay there chuckling at myself, enthralled with these tiny little pink and blue flowers protruding up from the green, soft moss that could not possibly be seen from a standing position.

What a wonderful find this place was. Had I only moments before taken my surroundings for granted? The beauty of this noble place took my breath away. Bright sunlight shone down through the treetops like little spotlights, brightly lighting fern and flower alike. Dying leaves floated down like little sinking ships, one here, one there, all over the scene. Life was abundant with the sounds and sights of little chattering rodents, peeping frogs and birds, that it was almost overwhelming. Such a different place this was than my sandy spit of land overlooking the cold blue friendless water. Not until that moment did I finally realize that I had made my escape from that lonely island prison and defeated death by the slightest margin. My god, it felt good to be alive!

Right then I didn't care if I was lost at all. My mind was at ease with the world, which seemed to be mine for the taking. I picked myself up, took a look at my compass, and continued my search for the hunters. As I braced myself one more time to conquer yet another fallen tree, I noticed I had put my hand in something that was cold, wet, and sticky. I looked at my hand and saw what I assumed was bright-red blood. I surmised it must have been the blood of whatever it was Maurice had shot, so off on the trail of blood I went. Tracking a blood trail is not an easy task. I had to carefully look for each crimson blotch. Sometimes it was on the forest floor, sometimes on a leaf or against the bark of a tree, but I did follow the trail. I tracked it right up to where the boys were. By the time I found the hunters, they were stuffing fresh deer meat into their packs. They had tracked the wounded deer until it was exhausted and losing its lust for life from loss of blood. The deer was mercifully dispatched with a knife to the throat, and within a short time, they managed to relieve the carcass of its meat with their large sharp hunting knives. I was amazed how easy it all seemed to be. Even more was the neatness with which they executed these actions. The leftover dear parts were piled and covered with pine boughs. The carcass was thrown over a high maple branch (to feed the birds, I was told). Everything else was shoved into large leather packs that were carried on their backs. I hardly had a moment's rest, and then we were off again. They had divided the meat into each pack so the loads would be carried evenly, and I hoped that the extra weight would slow them down, but that was not to happen. I did my best to keep up but found I was no match for the strength they seemed to have no end of.

They repeated this hunting episode twice that excruciatingly long day and shot the third deer while it was eating on the edge of a small clearing next to a large duck-filled pond. Beavers had slowed the flow of a creek and created this pond by erecting one of their powerful dams across its middle. Here was yet another beautiful scene in the midst of this gigantic forest. It was as if the hunters knew there was going to be something eatable in that clearing, because they approached the spot with guns raised and backpacks left behind on the ground. I watched this beautiful grazing whitetail creature receive the bullet right square in the chest and drop immediately, straight to the ground, as if its legs were made of rubber. Something must die so something else can live.

It was decided that we would camp there that night, owing to the fading light. I looked at my timepiece that showed it was after five in the evening. My pain-wracked body gratefully received the news that we were stopping for the night. I watched as the hunters turned to butchers, skillfully removing the best of the animals' meat and separating most of it from the bones. After this long day, there was little strength left in me. I felt stupid that I had forgotten to bring at least a small piece of canvas to wrap myself in for the night, but a thoughtful Frederic used his big hunting knife to slash enough balsam boughs to shelter me from the ground as well as from the sky. I could see why these men were fully clothed in buckskin. Buckskin was waterproof, tear proof, and soft, but made for comfortable night-clothes as well and was somewhat impervious to the cold. Each one of their outfits was sewn differently. The skin shirts had long tails and were slit and braided at the bottoms. Handstitched emblems and flowers and such adorned their outfits and made each of them look individual. It was very lovely handiwork to my eyes.

That evening we spent next to a comforting fire as I listened to Maurice interpret stories these men told of their families and homes. I sat on the ground eating deer meat that was pierced through with a sharpened stick and cooked over the hot flames then generously salted when it was done. After we ate, they shared a long clay pipe filled with the inner bark of the willow tree mixed with dried sumac leaves and tobacco with me. They called it Kinnikinick. We smoked the somewhat pleasant-tasting mixture while silently passing the pipe in a circle, one to the other. This we did several times over the course of the evening.

I learned that these men were the descendants of French voyagers and fur traders and had kept their own language and traditions. Their ancestors had come from France many years past, hired by Jesuit explorers, and had brought their colorful lifestyles to this new continent. Many stayed when the fur trade died and the Jesuits had gone home. All three of these good fellows migrated from the French-speaking province of Quebec for better money and shorter winters. As I sat watching and listening and dreaming of the beauty of their lives, I couldn't help but think that their way of life was even now disappearing with the onset of civilization and science. Men like this would soon be replaced by men who raised cattle and sheep for a living. Civilization was on the march. To my new friends, a telephone was only something they had heard about, yet the gates of civilization were but a slight way off.

Trapping and hunting had become profitable for the hunter when the lumber camps moved into the Canadian wilderness. Providing many loads of fresh meat required by the hardworking lumbermen was a full-time job and a healthy, hardy life. They spoke of their many children with pride. They also told me of the remaining camps of Chippewa Indians who welcomed their presence with open arms. Sometimes the trio would hire Indian men to help deliver their bounty to the rail tracks, and they paid the Indians well in return for being allowed to hunt on their ancestral lands. Even though the native population had been told in no uncertain terms the land now belonged to the King of England, the Chippewa treated the land as if it were their own, with the same respect their forefathers had given it generation upon generation. These savvy Frenchmen knew how to bridge what seemed like an enormous distance between the lumber camp bosses, the Canadian Mounted Police, and the noble and proud Indian nation. I found myself listening to their stories with awe and admiration.

It was all I could do that evening to make an entry into my daily log. The strong tobacco mix must have sent my head spinning because as I lay down on my pine-bough bed, their low-toned conversation rocked me into a dream. Their words flowed over me like the warm glow from the fire, heating everything its light touched. Words spoken in soft French turned into brightly colored whiffs of smoke that curled around my body and seemed to lift me into the air where, I remained suspended, locked in slumber until the morning noises replaced my wonderful dreams.

The forest echoed with the songs of a hundred birds. Dew dripped from a leaf hanging over my head and onto my face, waking me up. Soft morning light bounced off everything that offered a reflective surface. I wiped the sleep from my waking face with gritty, dirty hands. Looking at my dry, cracked, and burned hands, palms, and backs, I thought how far I had come and wondered when I would finally get home. Leafy refuse stuck to my shaggy hair as I surveyed the camp to see that I was there alone. I had slept soundly indeed, for I hadn't even heard the hunters depart, leaving the meat-filled packs behind in my trust, a sign that they would return.

I was hungry but felt little strength to move, so I pulled hard biscuits and some fish jerky from my bag and opened my canteen for a drink of yesterday's water. Crunching the biscuit and pulling on jerky, I saw there was a sandy beach leading into the pond near me. It was warm, and the sun was shining on the water, so I decided to take a bath and shake this dust off my stiff and aching body. Every fifty-four-year-old joint in my body said good morning to me as I lifted myself from my slumber pad and walked toward the swimming hole that beautiful morning. From the shade of the woods into the clear day's sunlight, the temperature rose considerably. The pond was larger than I originally thought. It was actually a well-formed lake. Off to the south, about sixty yards away, was a moose grazing the grassy lake bottom while standing in what would have been chest deep water for me. He lifted his massive head and gave little notice of me before plunging his head and antlers back under to rip another mouthful of swamp grass off the bottom. Stripping to my under-shorts and tiptoeing in, I found the water to be clear and, though chilly, quite pleasant. I was so completely enjoying my leisurely swim that I ventured far out into the lake. I breast-stroked and floated on my back, spitting plumes of water high over my head, like a whale might be seen doing at sea. Shortly, a chill built in me, and I had turned back toward the beach when I suddenly became aware that I was not alone.

There, sniffing at my clothes, were two scraggily looking coyotes. Several more were behind them in a group, and before I knew, it they had sniffed out the packs full of meat and were already trying to figure how to get into the heavy leather satchels. This happened so fast that I figured they must have been hiding, watching me and waiting for their opportunity to strike. The curs had somehow not noticed my presence in the water or else they didn't care. I elected to swim under the water and see if there was any chance I could get to my sack and my Colt revolver in time to save the meat from these would-be poachers. How would these hunters feel about me if I did nothing and allowed their booty to be dragged off by a pack of scrawny dogs? I lifted my head out of the water for a breath of air and saw one of the beasts pick up my pants and trot away with them, pant legs dragging behind him. If it hadn't been my pants, I might have thought it amusing, but they were my pants, and I found no humor in this at all.

I crawled from the water and up into the tall grass near our camp, where I could get a better look. This was a strange variety of coyotes. Too small to be from the wolf family, they looked more like dogs than the well-defined coyotes I had known in the past. One of these wild dogs was sniffing and sniffing the large packs, each of which must have weighed seventy or eighty pounds. They were stacked one on top of two, leaning against a tree with valuable antlers sticking out the top of each.

Just ten feet from the meat was my backpack lying on the ground next to where I had slept. I counted seven coyotes, including the one that was investigating my trousers. The largest and most dominant one was alternately biting at the bottom packs then snarling and snapping at the others to keep them away. Suddenly a fight erupted amongst some of the obviously hungry beasts, so while they were occupied elsewhere, I bounded to my feet and ran dripping wet for my bag and my weapon. I was surprised by my own agility, because it seemed like I dove eight or ten feet through the air to reach that bag before the canines realized I was there. I hit the ground and rolled into a sitting position with dirt and leaves sticking uncomfortably to my wet body. I already had my hand in the bag and on the gun's pearl handle before they fully realized my intrusion into their disordered world.

At first they took a fearful crouching startled position, and it looked like they would scatter, but one of the smaller beasts began to creep toward me with its head menacingly low and its back in a full bristle. My plan had been a hasty one, and my next move would have to be thought out better. I did not want to shoot an animal, but I would if I had to.

I had never owned a dog as a child, but I always wanted to. I knew that man had once domesticated these creatures, so I felt sure my superior mind would prevail in this situation. I stood up to look larger and more menacing to them, then slowly inched my way, in a sideways shuffle, until I was standing in front of the carrion-filled bags, but this persistent little cur followed my every move. While one was apparently interested only in me, the rest regained their composure and returned their attention to the bounty of fresh meat that unfortunately had a human standing between them and it. For a moment, I began to doubt the wisdom of my plan. What if I did shoot one of these creatures? Was there any guarantee the rest would disperse? Just how many bullets had I put in this old gun?

The complete memory of this situation is not clear; it all happened so fast. I knew I was in trouble but experienced no fear under the circumstances. No fear, which is, until I had made the decision to fire the pistol into the air and hopefully scatter the creatures in all directions. I lifted that trusted old revolver over my head, pointed it upward and on an angle toward the lake (so that the bullet wouldn't fall back to earth and land on my head). With confidence and security that the situation would be well in hand, I slowly squeezed the trigger. My finger squeezed and squeezed until I wasn't sure the trigger would work at all. Then I felt it trip and release the cocked hammer to fall on the bullet with what turned out to be a resounding *click*! A loud hissing, fizzing, popping sound was heard above me as I felt something hot and stinging hit my hand. My gun had misfired, and the lead bullet was stuck in the barrel! There was white smoke everywhere. I was so surprised to witness this event, having never seen this sort of thing happen before, that I forgot the dogs and inspected my rather hot and smoky firearm.

My next sensation was a searing pain as that one scrawny little snarling beast reached out and ran its claws down the full length of my bare leg. The whole smoky, sizzling, searing mess hadn't frightened it at all. There was no need to look down at my leg, because the feeling of blood slipping out of my skin needed no explanation. In a natural reaction, I threw that hot, useless gun straight at the coyote and luckily hit it square between the eyes. The dog yowled loudly and ran away. Fortunately a few of its cursed relatives, sensing its weakness, promptly pounced on it and began tearing that howling critter to shreds.

There I was in the middle of a full-blown feeding frenzy, and I had no weapon at hand. I saw a four-foot piece of tree branch sticking out from our firepit. I picked it up in a dash away from the tempting meat. I began to swing it wildly at the pack of dogs that took no time in letting go of their victim and concentrate on following after me. This action had startled the rest of the dogs into returning their attentions to me. Now it was me, and not the meat, they were after. I was now their query, and short of fighting each one of these snapping demons, I could see no way out of this predicament.

One of the coyotes lunged at me, and I struck it soundly in the ribs with my heavy log. It yelped and tumbled away in a roll but was replaced by another and another until I was swinging and hitting wildly at these creatures. One got hold of my calf from behind, and I struck it with such force I think I crushed its skull. It went to the ground at my feet and lay twitching and screaming violently. Then another lunged at me and knocked the log from my hand as I lifted it to block the dog's advance. I reached down to retrieve the log, but the attack was so fierce I was forced to hit at the dogs with my fists and feet instead. I was getting bitten on the arms and legs, and then I went down! There I was, on my bottom, yelling and kicking and throwing dirt and anything else I could grasp. Screaming "Get away! Get away!" as loud as I could and scurrying like a crab. On all fours, I crossed the ground toward a tree that I hoped I could scale.

I bumped into the tree and pressed my back up against it. I pushed my back up until I was standing once again. This was it! Now or never! I lunged for the first branch I could reach and caught it. I began pulling myself up, and for a second, I was safe. Then one of the attackers barely bit me on the backside and ended up hanging on me with a mouthful of my heavy cotton underpants in its grasp. I remember my reaction well. Being bitten by forty-pound dog creatures didn't bother me as much as the idea of sitting in a tree, naked and meatless, until my hunting companions returned to free me. I let go of the branch, bounced to the ground, and grabbed at the waist of my shorts to do battle for my dignity. It was as if the other dogs knew this was the deciding fight, because they seemed to stand back and watch as I pummeled at this creature while trying to turn on him for a face-to-face combat.

Smashing at him one handed and breaking my skin against his menacing teeth, I could gain no ground. He refused to let go and shook so violently that bracing myself against a fall was all I could do. I saw one of the buttons that went up the front of the shorts fly off in a great arc into the dirt where one of the other creatures seized it and ran away with it. I heard a ripping sound as my heavy cotton shorts began to tear, but then I heard a much louder tearing sound. It sounded as if the very tree I was standing under was splitting in two. It was a terrible sound that I didn't understand until I felt the coyote let go and fall to the ground with a gunshot wound to its head. My companions had returned and fired their rifles all at once, each at a different creature, leaving four dead coyotes, including the one I had killed, lying in a circle around me. They stepped into our camp and cautiously looked for the rest of the pack, but the survivors had long since departed. I stood there confused, covered in dirt and blood, stinging with bites and sweat, spinning around looking for errant coyotes and, of course, my pants, which I subsequently found in the brush.

As I hopped about the dusty camp with one leg in my pants and the other leg doing anything it could to keep my shaky body standing, my companions were laughing hilariously at me and stripping down for a swim themselves. I decided to join them in the water to survey and washed my wounds, finding they were more nuisances than life-threatening. Maurice told me that those creatures were a cross of coyotes and sled dogs that had been released into the wild by their owners once the railroad had opened their line, making the dog trails obsolete. There was a considerable bounty on each dog hide brought in because these animals had shown aggressiveness toward humans and were causing much trouble with the settlers. From the stories I heard told there, I had been lucky.

Before I could even get my bearings, Frederic had three of the dogs skinned and was working on the fourth. His skill with a knife was astounding. It was the skill of a craftsman who never thought of what it actually took to do his craft. It would have taken me hours to do what he did in just minutes. He probably gained this skill long before he was even in puberty.

The dog carcasses were left at the edge of the clearing in a pile, while the skins were put on a litter that Frederic had hastily built out of balsam saplings and leather twine. He had woven a pattern of twine between two six- or seven-foot poles lashed apart by a three-foot stick on the bottom. Then he laid the skins on and placed several piles of twine-wrapped deer meat on top. This was a good way of spreading the load so a man could carry more than his back could endure. With his bright-colored sash lashed to the poles for a harness, John Paul gave me his lightened pack of meat, while he took the litter for himself. I carried my new pack, with the unusable pistol in it, on my front. For the first time, I felt useful to these men, and it gave me some pride to do so. This was their life, and to them, my attack was but part of the day.

We packed up the camp and did what it took to get our minds back on track. I was wounded, bleeding, and somewhat confused, but I did what I could to help get the meat-filled packs on the hunters' and my backs. I remember being the last to leave the clearing in a procession of men with deer antlers sticking out of their packs, looking like they were sporting antlers themselves. Looking back to the clearing as we entered the narrow path that followed the stream from the beaver pond, which strangely enough was flowing north, I saw that it was a place which I was sure had been used by humans before and would probably be used by humans again. It would be a familiar place to my memory and not soon forgotten.

As usual, I had to work to keep up, but this time it was a little easier to do so. I had learned their cadence, and their heavier loads did not seem to slow them down a bit. My own load had become part of my body as if it were some sort of large hump that I had carried all my life. It took little time for me to forget all that was around me and fall into a mechanical pace that seemed to stretch my breath and strength as well. With me mostly looking toward the ground and following close behind, I was surprised when the party came to a halt after what was less than an hour's march. The path mostly followed along a good-sized stream that seemed to drop over rock formations every hundred yards or so. We had been descending steadily, and I was thankful it wasn't climbing we were doing instead.

As I looked up, I could see that they had stopped where the stream spilled quietly into a lake. It was a beautiful lake, with tall pine trees hugging it all around. Following their lead, I took my pack off and laid it on the ground next to theirs. The three hunters went up a small rise and started to uncover a manmade pile of pine boughs that revealed canoes lying on the ground beneath them. I had not noticed the pile of pine until the boys began uncovering it, and I was surprised to see three birch-bark canoes lying there on the ground.

Maurice told me that the water was the shortest way to the rail line where they would meet the train. He said that they would travel this way, coming to the lake and taking their canoes north, then it was just a short walk to the place where the train would stop for them. After unloading their bounty on the train, they would return to the canoes and repeat their trek in the opposite direction, eventually returning home for a well-deserved rest. Again these men had surprised me with their limitless utility.

I was assigned a spot in the largest canoe with Maurice, who leapt in, managing to not even get a toe wet as he pushed off the pebbly beach into that beautiful lake. I was put in the bow and clumsily tried to help in the rowing and kick off my soaking-wet boots at the same time. There was little wind, and within a short time, the two of us had the paddling down. Maurice could have done the job himself, but I assured myself that I was giving him at least some slight advantage. We traveled side by side across the lake in a somewhat more easterly direction with a small wave breaking off each canoe bow, as we made for somewhere on the opposite shore. I was happy to be a part of this, knowing that I would never have seen this beauty on my own. The scene was so large and so unspoiled in its grandeur that I felt privileged beyond belief. I was indeed a very lucky man.

I had no idea whether this enormous lake even had a name, but that didn't stop me from feeling the exhilaration the explorers of old must have felt each time they found something new. My lust for that feeling was what had kept me sailing about and following previously beaten paths, but here in this pristine spot, I may have been the first "outsider" ever to see this. Of course this was unlikely, but I allowed myself to dream.

When we reached the other shore, the canoes fell into line, one behind the other, and entered a narrow opening into a marshy area that nestled between islands of hemlock and rock. This was yet another natural path the hunters would follow. It flowed one way then the other through tall grass, sometimes switching back so much that we passed each other going in opposite directions. Finally the marsh opened up into a large expanse of grassy, wildlife-filled wonderland. Amphibious fowl and beaver, moose and bear, all kinds of wildlife were within my view in and around that beautiful place. Bird song filled the air with a symphony of nature that could lull even the worst of us into a blissful joy. In some spots, the grass was so high I had no idea what might lay ahead of us. I was at the head of the procession and must have looked like a little kid as my head swung from side to side in absolute wonderment. Then as the vista cleared into a marsh and we entered an area that was less confined, there in front of me were several more canoes filled with people.

"Miiqwech!" I heard Maurice shout.

"Miiqwech!" was the reply from no less than five canoes that seemed to just spring up from the tall grass.

We paddled into the midst of these canoes and were greeted by smiling round-faced Indian people who talked back and forth, speaking what I assumed was Chippewa. We had come on them as they were pushing their canoes with long poles through the shallow grassy water, harvesting wild rice. It was one of their major staples and had been harvested every fall for as long as man had been around. All their activity had stopped, and the conversations began as we approached. There were handshakes and hugs from one canoe to another. To me it looked like a family reunion, which it may have been for all I knew.

Amazingly, I was completely ignored. It was as if I weren't there at all. No explanation was offered for my presence, and apparently none was asked for. The only time I was even noticed was when I had to hold on to the Indian canoe while the two civilizations exchanged meat for rice, and that was nothing but shallow glances. This was strange to me, though I did realize that my attire must have seemed quite strange to their eyes. I was later to learn that, had I been introduced, it would have called for a feast that the hunters just didn't have the time for.

Before we parted their company, something else I found strange happened. Each canoe came up to the canoe Maurice and I were in, and each person in those canoes made a point of touching what looked like a bear-claw hanging by a leather thong from Maurice's neck. There must have been fifteen natives, and each one closed their hand around the claw for a moment. Maurice sat silent and motionless. For the life of me, I could not imagine what was going on. I had seen this claw when first I met Maurice, but I hadn't given it a second thought.

I felt strange as we paddled away because everyone was waving goodbye except for me. I had made no new friends and had no idea what had just happened. As soon as we were out of earshot, Maurice offered his apologies. He wasted no time in explaining that, because I was traveling and hunting with them, the Chippewa people would greet me as a brother, and they would insist in initiating me into their tribe, a process that took many days to complete. I was saddened that I had lost this incredible opportunity, but they had to deliver the meat while it was still fresh, and I was anxious to get back to civilization and inform my wife that I was still alive. I could only imagine what wonders I would have experienced at the hands of those handsome people. I pondered this disappointment for a while and then remembered what had happened with Maurice's claw necklace. I asked him what that was all about, and he explained that the claw was indeed a bear claw, but a very special and sacred one. I looked at it when he held it out for my inspection, and I could see that it was pure white and looked almost like it was made from ivory. The claw had belonged to Maurice's grandfather, and the old man had come about it in a very strange way. It seemed that the grandfather, whose name was also Maurice, was a trapper working for the Hudson Bay Company. He would go out into the wilds of Canada and trap every summer, not to return to Fort Francis until fall each year. There, he would be paid for his hard work and then supply himself for the long Canadian winter.

The story began when Maurice's grandfather bought a birch bark canoe from some Indians on the Nippagon flowage. The problem was that these Indians had no knowledge of buying and selling things in their culture. In the tribe, everything was shared, and everything they had belonged to all. The old man offered them tea and tobacco for the canoe, but they apparently thought that the elder Maurice was just borrowing it, giving tea and tobacco for the consideration. The trapper loaded his packs and headed out onto the river for a trek upstream where the beaver were thick. A couple of the young braves followed the man up the river at a respectful distance so as not to inhibit him. When old Maurice pulled the canoe up on the shore and walked away from it with his gun and trapping gear, they naturally thought he was done with the canoe, so they took it and returned home. They never thought twice about what they had done.

Maurice's grandfather was furious when he discovered the canoe was gone. He went back to the camp and demanded that they give him back the canoe. His bold insistence incensed the tribe, and the chief had the Frenchman summarily thrown into the river. Old Maurice was even madder than the chief, so he waited outside the camp until the time was right, then snuck back in and stole the canoe back from the Indians. He felt that he had done the just thing but was afraid of their reprisal, so he took to hiding the canoe carefully every time he left it, and this is where the bear claw comes in.

The story goes that Maurice went through great effort to hide the canoe from sight and would go so deep into a thicket to do so that sometimes he would get stuck trying to get himself out. One of these times he got stuck in muck and bramble so thick he could hardly move. As luck would have it, in the commotion he disturbed a cantankerous old black bear that was eating blueberries right there in the thicket. Usually the black bear is a gentle animal, so shy it will run away from a human, but this one was a different sort and did his best to kill and eat Maurice's grandfather. The bear dragged the screaming and thrashing trapper out of the thicket and thoroughly tore him up. Just when the trapper thought his end was near, something almost supernatural happened. From out of absolutely nowhere, a pure white bear came to the rescue. It was an albino bear with bright-red eyes, a shiny white coat, and glistening white teeth, and that pure white bear chased the black bear clean away. The old trapper was powerfully hurt and could not stand up much less run, but he watched as the white bear stood up and held its ground against a larger and more ferocious cousin, facing him down without a fight. The black bear turned tail and slowly sauntered off, leaving the dying man alone with this white apparition.

The old man didn't know if what he saw was real or if it was just part of dying, but he did feel the bear lift him up by his coat and drag him over to the cold water's edge, where the bear shoved him with his strong pink nose right into the water, up to the old man's neck, and then the bear sat there watching the bleeding man until the man's eyes closed and his consciousness faded away.

Legend has it that the bear stayed with the man for the better part of a week and kept him safe from other predators. Old Maurice managed to gain enough strength to pull the canoe out of the rough by a rope that was attached to the bow and push it into the water after many days of near starvation. All the time that white bear stayed nearby and gave the old man no indication that he would be further harmed. As he rolled over the gunnel into the canoe, drifting from the shore, he saw the bear walk into the water and loudly roar out a call to the wild. The canoe drifted, as he thought it would, right up to the Indian village, where he was well cared for until his body repaired. The Indians had no malice for a man who needed their help and gave him every consideration they could possibly give. Their medicine worked well, and the man was up and walking within a few months. He returned their favor a hundredfold just by telling them the story of his encounter with the great white bear. To them this was strong medicine and meant that the tribe would be under the bear's protection and would prosper. Many of the tribe went to find the bear and leave him gifts of apples and wild berries and jewelry.

It was good that the bear was there for the Indian, but it turned out to be bad for the bear. The word of the medicine bear had gotten out into the European world, and it was no time before white men put the bear into their sights in hopes of earning a fortune for its hide. One such man was a grizzled old trapper named Buffalo. He was as big as his name and had an extreme love for his solitude. A more unsociable man may never have roamed North America. Not many people cared for the man, and he could have cared less if they did.

I listened to this story as we entered yet another lake and began crossing it. As I swung my paddle from one side to the other, the story unfolded in a stream of pictures of times gone by. It was a story that might have been listened to with a skeptic's ear if I hadn't seen the ivory white claw for myself. Maurice obviously was proud of his affiliation with this history and continued his story as we headed over the open water.

The grandfather feared for his lifesaving friend the bear and let it be known far and wide that the white bear was not to be harmed. Not only was the bear sacred to the Indians, but there was a white man who thought the bear to be supernatural also. Old Maurice was so bold as to let it be known that he would not hesitate to kill the man who harmed his bear, and he took a public oath with his hand on a Bible to prove it. It was fairly well-known that he meant the threat and all would respect his word. All, that is, except old Buffalo. Buffalo would hunt the bear because he knew the reward would be great. Not the thought of financial reward, but the knowledge that he would be known as the man who bagged the great white bear. He would be a legend, and ultimately, that is what he wanted to be. Buffalo wanted to be a legend, and there was nothing else that would occupy his mind from the time he heard about the existence of this great bear somewhere in his world.

Maurice's grandfather had heard of Buffalo's threat to kill his bear, and he took it very seriously. The two men had met many times in the past, and like so many who met Buffalo, Maurice did not like him. Maurice set out to find the trapper and warn him personally not to shoot the white bear, but he was too late. The man they called Buffalo had stalked and shot the great white bear. He had killed the supernatural spirit that protected the good people and the land around them.

My newfound companion was filled with emotion as he continued the tale. He stammered slightly as he emotionally recounted what his grandfather had done then. As we paddled on, he went on to say the following:

"Grandfather found Buffalo camped not too far from where he had been attacked by the black bear. There, sitting draped in the furs of many animals he had killed, was this loathsome man. Grandfather wandered into the camp on foot and could see the great white hide, head and all, stretched from tree to tree and scraped clean of all its flesh. Grandfather lifted his rifle and, without a word, shot the man dead, right through the heart, with one clean shot, while the bastard sat there chewing on a piece of fresh killed bear meat."

Maurice went on to tell me that his grandfather loaded the hide onto Buffalo's packhorse and took everything the man owned to the Indian village, leaving Buffalo's naked body on the ground for the wild animals to take their revenge on. There he gave it all to the chief and began to leave the village carrying a very heavy heart. It was then that the chief stopped him and asked him to stay and become one of the tribe, which the grandfather of Maurice gladly did. When he left the village many years later, he was with his new wife, Maurice's grandmother, and he was wearing the great white's bear claw around his neck. It was the very one that he gave his grandson so many years later.

"This is that very same bear claw, and to this day it symbolizes how great the bear was and also how great was the man that avenged its death." He held the claw up toward the sky with his eyes looking to a heaven that only he could see. I had listened with much interest to this story and felt proud that he had shared it with me. Maurice had made me part of this wilderness by telling me this thing. I felt close to the place that I was in and crossing over with such an abundance of history to share. We have the day to live, then that day turns into the history of that day. Some times and some places provide very interesting stories, to be sure.

Within a few hours, we left the lake and pulled the canoes up and covered them in the same way we found them when we began. We loaded back up and returned to our walk. As we walked, I thought of the story I had just been told and forgot all about what I was doing until I began to get hungry. I was sure we would not stop until we reached our goal, so I took a swig of lake water from my canteen. The taste was sweet indeed. As sweet as the day that was bright and full of wonder.

By early that evening, we had arrived at the rail clearing they had told me about. I saw nothing but one set of tracks with barrels and stacks of bundles of furs and such. Firewood was piled there also; I assumed it was to be used as fuel for the engine fires. There was no sign of human life, but it was obvious this was a place where humans congregated and carried on commerce. We arrived carrying not only the packs full of meat and antlers but also a litter stacked with fresh kill and the four dog hides. Camping there for the night brought me a feeling of sadness because of the realization that I would be leaving these wonderful new friends early the next morning. Working and walking with these men had given me a strength I could not have given myself, even in my isolation time. I envied their total independence and their closeness to and understanding of nature.

Their attention to my wounds was punctuated with a show of scars and holes they each had earned for themselves in the wild. To them, being bitten or even shot was all part of the day's work. They slept longer than I did the next morning, and as I sat watching the sun add dimension to the day, I surveyed my life and thought how wonderful each breath of this incredible freedom actually was. That morning I would gladly have traded the sea for the woods. At that point in my adventure, I began to see a different way of life through these men. To be able to sleep on the ground and find one's daily sustenance in the wild, while at the same time supporting a family, was nothing less than admirable. Their pay was trust, and their trust was well founded. None would dare cheat these men of their due.

As they woke, each in his turn, I watched them quietly guiding themselves through some ritual or another. John Paul stoked the fire and walked to the creek for water to make the coffee. Frederic, though he had slept on the ground with no cover against the cold and dew, stood up and shook off the night like a dog might have done. He let his hair down from a bun that he wore on the back of his head and pulled a shell comb from his pouch and raked it through it. Maurice never moved from his perch until he had lit the pipe and pulled on what was left from the night before. None of them said a word, and I sat on my heels, enjoying the silence and serenity of their lives.

Without looking at anything but the sun for their awareness of time, the hunters started to break camp just moments before we heard the sound of a train's whistle blowing in the distance. Shortly, there was a modest steam-and-smoke-belching locomotive with one coach, three old boxcars, and an empty flat car with an old unpainted caboose on the end, steaming to a stop in the clearing. The engine was of a smaller variety than I was used to seeing in the States. It looked foreign to me, but of course, I was in a foreign land. As the train jerked with a succession of clangs, a stealthy old gentleman jumped from the still-moving train and jogged in an easy gait toward us. Wearing a conductor's cap with the Canadian National Railway's insignia on it, his gray hair did not match the ease of his stride. He greeted the three woods-dwelling Frenchmen as old friends do and looked toward me while Maurice pointed at me and apparently told him the story of the dog-bitten American castaway who fell down from the sky. The old conductor laughed hardily, as they had laughed, and reached for my hand to shake it vigorously. He shook his head as if in disbelief as he took the sack from my back.

The hunters stacked the meat in the boxcar and then covered it with the dog hides. They each took a slip of paper from the conductor, which I assumed showed that their transaction was done. They seemed pleased and smiled at each other as they shared a glance at their respective receipts. I heartily shook my new friends' hands, looking each one in the eye with gratitude, and waved goodbye as I entered the coach. My affinity for these men surprised me. I felt a pang of regret that I hadn't gotten to know them better or at least exchanged addresses. But these men were not the sort to communicate or even to travel, for that matter. If I was ever to see them again, it would have to be by my own volition.

I was ushered into what looked like an old passed-down coach that was also filled with a verity of freight. Its wheels were small and close together, and the car looked too tall, as if it would fall off the tracks in a sharp turn. Standing in the doorway as we pulled away from that clearing, I saw that my friends did not seem in such a hurry anymore. Instead they waited by the tracks, watching and waving until we were almost out of sight. I made a feeble attempt to bid farewell in French by yelling, "Au revoir!"

To this day, I do not understand the French language. At my last sight of them, they were shouldering their rifles and packs, walking back toward the forest to resume their duties. I have often wondered what would have happened if they had actually gotten my balloon off the ground. If they were successful, they might have changed the history of Canada. The image of them hunting from the air was hilarious to me. The image of them putting the contraption together and using it amused me greatly. I hoped they would.

The little train's conductor's name was Samuel, and he sported a fine western American drawl. I learned that he had come by it by growing up in Montana. Samuel was tall, over six feet, and sported a fine white mustache that covered his lips to the point of distraction when he talked to me. I found myself staring at his mouth, looking for the place the words were coming from. He was an American who found himself living and working in Canada after his dream of finding gold in Ontario had dried up. When he mentioned the gold, I was embarrassed to realize that I had given no thought to money. I had to make him a promise to pay when I made arrangements to get some, for my money had been absentmindedly left in a tent on Montreal Island. He was very willing to take me at my word, having had a formal introduction from the hunters and all, so that was that.

Conversation with Samuel was enjoyable. He had a wit and flair for conversation that left me laughing heartily. Eating had not been a priority that day, so I found myself hungry, which Samuel took care of by sharing his lunch of sausage and French bread with me. When he went about his duties, which was sorting the mail, I felt alone and strangely nervous for it. I could see that my adjustment to civilization was not going to be that easy. As we chugged to a speed that sometimes seemed too much for these tracks, I rested against a bale of what appeared to be bearskins and dreamed of the great adventure I had just enjoyed. The life of a woodsman is as pure as anything a human can experience. Life in the woods is much like life at sea, with the need to rely on one's self for survival. I laughed as I thought of the hunters finding a clearing and trying to make my airship fly once again. What if they were successful? It could truly change history.

T HE RIDE TO the Sault started out as an enjoyable one, with several outback stops along the way where I saw a mix of Native
Indian people and Europeans as well as Americans looking for a new
life or perfecting the one they had here. It was quite a pleasant ride,
until one stop, where two red-coated policemen mounted on beautiful black horses were escorting a handcuffed and struggling, unde-
sirable-looking man toward the train. Samuel spoke at length with
them, and from what I could understand, it was decided that this
man would be riding in the car with me. In fact, one of the officers
entered my coach and asked me if I would be willing to guard this
man until we arrived at Sault Ste. Marie. I had enjoyed the solitude
and rest that was an amendment to me being alone. I was finding
that traipsing uninterrupted through my thoughts and jotting things
down into my log was somewhat therapeutic. I had not noticed how
stressed I had been until, once again, I found myself in solitude. My
hope had been to quietly enjoy the ride and possibly catch some
sleep, but when asked to help by one of Canada's finest, I felt compelled to assist in any way I could. "What would you have me do?"
I asked.

"I understand you possess a pistol," he answered.

"Yes, sir, but it doesn't work, and there is a bullet stuck in the
barrel."

"Monsieur La Chance does not know that," he said as he raised
his hands in gestured surprise.

La Chance, eh. I was somehow talked into allowing myself to be a prison guard for the remaining three or four hours it would take to get to Sault Ste. Marie. Other policemen would meet the train and relieve me of my burden when we arrived there. I was not happy with this turn of events but figured I should do my bit.

Mr. La Chance was ushered in and manacled to a seat at the rear of the car. The police officer handed me the keys to the locks that held him, and I stuck them in my shirt pocket. He thanked me and turned to leave. This was all happening too fast, and I was not sure what it was I had gotten into. "What has this man done?" I somewhat shouted to his back.

"Sir, this is a very bad man indeed. It would be easier to tell you what he has not done than what he has done."

"What if he tries to escape?" I asked.

The officer turned toward the wretched, snarling prisoner, looked him square in the eyes, and said in French, "Abattez 'le." Then he turned to me and said, "Shoot him dead." Then he winked and left me alone with Mr. La Chance. Shoot him with a gun that doesn't work. Now there's a novel idea. I hadn't taken time to clear the bullet from the sulfur-stained gun barrel, and if I had to point it at him, he would surely see the lead slug stuck in the end of that old Colt revolver. Just so Mr. La Chance knew I had the gun, I stood and walked over to where Samuel had put my pack and slowly and deliberately removed the gun from the sack, never taking my eyes off my prisoner once.

This man's gaze unsettled me a bit. I got the same feeling I had when being stalked by that one nasty little dog. He watched my every move, and aside from his stone-cold black eyes and a few white teeth, his face was completely covered by a coal-black beard that had obviously not been cut in many years. His hair went everywhere and curled down to meet his beard in a black mess. The mass of hair and beard made him look as if there was just a head, with no shoulders, attached to what I could now see was a massive body. Returning to my bearskin perch, with nothing but some flimsy chain and a useless revolver between him and me, I began to think this was not such a good idea. Somehow I knew that this man was not going to quietly sit here, in this two-man environment, winding through the Canadian wilderness, and not try to escape. I began to think about what I would do if I were in his pace. Lacking completely the criminal mentality, I thought about the lust for freedom and how far this man might go to obtain it. Would he be willing to kill me in order to get it? Was he a murderer? Had I, by a quirk of chance, been thrust into a most dangerous position? I had to assume all these questions would be answered in the affirmative. A cold sweat broke out on my face, which I immediately wiped away lest he sense my growing fear. I had successfully put myself in a quandary over something I didn't even know to be true. For all I knew, he might have been a sheep rustler.

I returned to my pack to gather my logbook and a scrap of bandage I could use to wipe the smoke from my gun. Once again the prisoner followed my every move. I knew this man's stock in trade must have required him to be proficient in intimidation. I was resolved not to allow this to happen to me. After all, he thought I had a working gun, and that would probably be enough to keep him at bay. Wiping the pistol down, I glanced at him from time to time, and every time I did, my eyes met his directly. This was unnerving, to say the least. He was staring at me and not removing his glare at all. It would be unwise for me to stare back at him, for I would surely lose the contest. I again began to feel a sweat rising up on my forehead. My mind raced with wild notions of a fight with this man and me the looser. What would I do if he did attempt an escape? Even if I mercifully freed him, what would be the guarantee he would not kill me just for the fun of it? I thought of my knife, but pulling it from my bag would surely tip my gunless hand and maybe give him a chance at a weapon. No doubt, I had backed my mind into a hell of a corner. Then I heard a noise. It was La Chance jerking his chain manacle harshly against the seat armrest he was shackled to. As he did this, he never removed his gaze from me. I looked to the seat nearest me and surveyed the construction. The seats were made of metal with wooden slats for the seats and backs. From the look of it, there was plenty of strength in the metal, and the bolts holding the seats together were sufficiently strong. If the situation wasn't bad enough, he began to say something to me in a language I felt sure was his own version of French-Canadian, which I had become familiar with over the last few days. This was the first time I felt less than uncomfortable looking at him. He was obviously asking a question, but I had no idea what he was saying.

"Boire?" was his word, and it was asked in such a way I knew it was a question.

"Boire?" he gestured with his cuffed hands, like drinking from a cup.

"Water?" I asked.

"Oui! Water!" he blurted at me.

I followed his look as he gestured toward the front of the car, where there was a large wooden cask, lying in a cradle, with a tin cup hanging from a spigot. I went over and investigated where, indeed, there was fresh water. I took a sip and found it to be very refreshing. I hadn't realized how thirsty I had become, and it took two full cups to quench my thirst. With the cup in my hand, I raised it in a questioning manner toward the wild man. He sheepishly nodded his head up and down, which was the signal for yes in any language. I poured him a cup and, feeling a slight kinship in thirst, started toward him. Then I realized the danger in getting that close to this mad criminal. All he had to do was grab me and extract the keys from my pocket and I was done. So I slowly inched toward his seat, calculating how close I could get before he could reach me. From an arm's length, I offered the cup, but this clever cur pretended to be chained closer than he was. His attempt was so obvious that I grinned and said, "Oh no you don't. You can reach for it."

He pretended again, and I stood patiently. I was the parent here. I was in charge, and I was not going to be fooled by this fiend. As I stood there, I caught a whiff of his odor. It was as wild as anything I had ever smelled. As a matter of fact, it was similar to the smell of the dead dogs we had skinned back at the pond. The dogs actually smelled better, because this creature had a definite smell of stale urine permeating his presence. I began to get a sickening feeling from this man and wanted to be done with this task as soon as possible. Suddenly, as I stood there steeping in repulsion, he jumped up and lunged toward me, thrusting his head at me with such force that it knocked the cup out of my hand, and his head hit me square in the middle of my chest, knocking me backward and down to the floor. Standing there, looking down at me, he attempted to kick me. Like a wild ape, he was kicking and growling and jerking at his chains with such brute force that I was afraid he might break free.

I got up and ran to my seat, where I grabbed my gun, and began to turn it on him. This gesture caused him to settle down somewhat. I hoped I was cautious enough not to point it straight at him because he might see the frozen bullet and realize the gun was useless. Once again I was faced with the prospect of throwing the gun at my opponent in order to use it as a weapon. I smarted in embarrassment that such a lout could surprise me in that manner but found some satisfaction in the fact that he caused me to spill the water, and there was no way I would get him more. What I didn't know was that the reason he settled down was not the threat of being blasted by this ancient mariner, for I am sure he had seen the gun was useless. Indeed, he had spotted the fact that the shackle keys had fallen out of my shirt pocket when he had head-butted me. Now he took on the air of a frightened child in an effort to relieve my anxiety, I suppose. He sat down, and for the first time, he bowed his head, taking his glare away from me. I was mistakenly under the impression the six-gun threat was working.

I also didn't know that Mr. La Chance was a thoroughly desperate man and had proven to be totally unmanageable in the past. After all, it had taken two big men just to get him onto the train. If I had known that he was feared and hated all across Canada, I would have refused to help. This man had quite a reputation, and few lived to tell the story of an encounter with Armand La Chance. The Mounties had put their trust in some chains and an old wooden and steel bench seat to keep the two of us separated. Now it had come down to that, plus the empty threat of a useless antique weapon being all that stood between my life and my death. But I didn't know that at the time.

I sat down with Mr. Colt's useless peacemaker lying across my lap. I watched him, wondering whether or not he would try something else. Unknown to me, the keys were laying only a few feet away from him, but he had no way of gathering them up. I know his mind was racing, because his freedom was only a little way off, and he had to retrieve the keys before I would realize they were gone. Now it was I who was doing the staring. I kept an eye on him as he pretended to try and nap. I knew there were hours until my relief, so I endeavored to relax as well. At that time though, I had no idea I was in real danger. Above the sting of the dog bites and scratches, aside from my very sore calf muscles, I now had a dull ache emanating from my bruised ribs freshly given to me by a brand-new adversary.

This stinking black-hearted villain was so clever. He stretched his legs out, one under the seat, and the other out in the aisle. What I didn't see was that he stretched to his limit, pointed his right moccasin-clad toe, and bent his ankle to the left until he felt the bump of the keys lying on the floor, all the time yawning and pretending to stretch. He somehow managed to scrape the keys under the seat and out of my sight, where he quietly slid them toward himself with his other foot. Right about that time, the little wilderness train began to enter a series of switch-backs. The engineer slowed the locomotive down as the turns became tighter. We were rising up over a series of hills, and as we crested each one, the brakes were set to allow a slow descent. The little train was bumping and pulling, then lurching and twisting, until I had to hang on or fall over.

The beauty of the scenery that was unfolding in front of my eyes was astounding. There, off to the west, was a panoramic scene of beautiful Lake Superior, edged by a stream- and ravine-cluttered forest that was showing the full radiance and colors of fall. My complete attention was on this incredible view. I was standing, facing forward, with my back to La Chance, which gave him a great opportunity to gather up the keys. He must have pinched the keys between his feet and lifted them until he could grab them with his hands. At any rate, he managed to quietly unlock the chain that held him to his seat and was in the process of freeing his hands when I turned to sit down.

As I nestled back into my seat, I could see a change in his demeanor. There he was, looking at me with that cold stare again. He was glaring with a new intensity, which immediately put me on my guard. Then, like a bolt of lightning, my mind reenacted the head-butt, and without thinking, I reached for the keys in my top pocket. My fingers felt nothing. and as quick as a gasp, I realized the keys were gone. The train suddenly braked as my eyes met La Chance's and, like a shot, before he could unlock his cuffs, he was out of his seat and lunging for me. I lifted my pistol, but it was too late to threaten him with it. He was on me, and from my seated position, I could find no way to escape. All I could do was throw the gun over my head and into the corner, hoping he would follow it and let me escape. I tried to roll off my seat and gain my feet, but La Chance was on me like that damn pack of dogs. This time the attacker was bigger and much more dangerous than before. There were no trees to climb. There was no way I could, from this position, escape the man. I rolled over, onto my back, and was struck squarely in the face with his big fist. He hit me again and again, and all I could do was try to cover my face with my arms in hopes he would cease this attack. My head was ringing, and my lips and nose were stinging from his blows, but then he lifted me by my hair and savagely wrapped his maniacal chain around my throat.

Without a second to realize my plight, he banged my head back to the floor violently and, with the strength of a madman, began to choke me with the chain. All I could do was grab at the chain with my fingers, but the force he was using would not allow me to get my fingers between my neck and the chain. The pain was excruciating, but more than that, I could not breathe in or out. I gasped, but no breath came. It all happened so fast that the reality of this situation didn't sink in until I became aware that this man was actually trying to kill me. I could not breathe, and I was helpless to fight. He was too heavy to move or throw off, so I swung my fists at him with all I had left, but my arms were too short to reach his face, and I succeeded only in lamely striking at his fully flexed arms. I felt all the strength draining from my body. My vision dimmed from a view of this insane killer's face looming over me into a white milky blur, with the sound of rail tracks passing beneath me prominent in my head. I was dying!

Sounds of steel wheels and steel brakes meeting each other on a downward slope, with steel tracks clapping as the wheels passed over their joints. The hiss of steam and the puff of the pistons rang in all that was left of my mind. All sight and sound began to blend into one little tangled, dreamlike thought. This was the end, and I had no time to regret it. Before the light started to go out, even though I was aware of an evil presence forcing life out of my body, I saw visions of water and boats and people, especially my wife, floating around in my thoughts. Then there was nothing. The sounds had gone away, and the light had gone out. The only sensation I had left was the feeling of something very heavy surrounding me. It was dark and quiet. Was I buried? Had I died and been put under the ground? My mind was working, or at least I could ask these questions. Was this the after-life?

Then I heard a sound. It was the sound of a voice, one that was familiar to me. It was Samuel, the conductor. "Partner, are you all right?"

The weight of something large was crushing me from above, and there was a putrid smell all around me. I opened my eyes and saw Samuel standing over me with what looked like a stick in his hand but turned out to be a lead-filled wooden club that he carried under his jacket for just such a situation. He had come into the car, caught La Chance on top of me, and rendered him unconscious with one solid blow to the back of his large, empty skull. The man was so massive that it took the two of us to lift him off me, though I was weak and of little assistance. As I sat there gasping and coughing, Samuel handed me a cupful of water, which I painfully drank. He was having a problem dragging the criminal over to the chains he had freed himself from, so I climbed over the lout and fetched the chains myself. We decided to chain him hand and foot, and leave him there on the floor, bundled in as uncomfortable a position as we could get him into.

Aside from more scratches, blood trickling from my lip and nose, bruised red and swollen cheeks, I was surprisingly unscathed. My throat was very sore, and I found it hard to swallow for a few days after, but other than that, I was all right. Actually, I became quite elated to realize how close I had come to dying and was so giddy with the knowledge I was alive that I made Samuel a promise to buy him all the whisky he could drink when we arrived at the Sault. He patted me on the back, politely declined, and carried on with his duties. I felt drunk and dizzy, I suppose from some burst of adrenaline or something, but at that moment I was euphoric with the knowledge that life is precious and mine had been spared. Samuel had taken the whole thing in stride, as if it was nothing, but indeed I owed this man my life! As my thoughts started to congeal again and sound and sight reentered me there on that little train, I experienced such clarity that everything I knew about life changed. Somehow, from that time on, I never looked at things the same again. Our last moment on this earth is but one little breath away. One short unknown breath that will be the last we will ever take. It is but a brief moment from now. Though I never have a thought of them, each and every unnoticed breath is precious, and from that day on, I was well aware of that fact. One more thing to give thanks for when my day was over, and I sent a humble thank you to my Creator.

I put the old Colt revolver back into my bag and gathered my pencil and logbook to write the incident down before I forgot it. By the time La Chance revived, with a series of agonizing groans, I was cleaning my fingernails with my sharp rigging knife. As the big ugly fool regained consciousness, he found me staring at him with a mincing grin, because, by that time, I would not have hesitated to use my knife on him if need be, and he knew it. I found much satisfaction watching him rub the back of his head then stare at the fresh blood that was sticking to his fingers.

We arrived in what the locals called the Sault, the town of Sault Ste. Marie, on the Canadian side of the St. Marys River just before dark. Samuel led me out to a group of waiting Mounties, where he told them of my near-death encounter with the man they were there to retrieve. It appeared, judging by the number of police there to pick La Chance up, and the battle he subsequently put up as they lead him off, that he was indeed a very dangerous man. One of the policemen told me that La Chance was being escorted to the local jail, and then he would be shipped off to the provincial prison, where he would spend the rest of his life behind bars for killing his own grandparents just to steal their meager savings. That knowledge sent a cold shiver up and down my spine. How close I had come!

As they dragged this man beast kicking and growling past me, he uttered something in his guttural language and spit in my direction. He seemed to be quite angry that I was still alive and must have blamed me for his continued incarceration. When I asked Samuel what the prisoner had said, he informed me that La Chance had cursed me and promised retribution. How he figured on doing that, I did not know.

The policeman was very polite and pointed the way to the local hotel, where he assured me I would be welcome. He made sure I was aware that someone would be by to see me in the morning so I could fill out a report on my unscheduled stop in his country and the one-sided fight with that human tree. Tall, with a remarkably square jaw, the policeman gave no doubt that he was the epitome of authority.

I shook Samuel's hand and thanked him for literally saving me from the jaws of death. With great sincerity, I promised to pay the stationmaster for my ride when I got my money, then we parted as friends forever. I stood there with his hand in mine and searched for the words that would convey to him my emotion and could find none. Samuel smiled and simply said, "Don't worry, partner, your turn will come to pay me back by saving someone else." Then a simple "Adios!" and that was that.

I strolled in the direction I was told would lead me to the hotel and became aware of the way people were looking at me. I must have been a sight! An unwashed, tattered, bleeding, and bruised old man, cut and bandaged all over, with wild, unkempt hair and a scraggily beard, carrying nothing more than a cloth bag over my shoulder and a leather-bound book in my hand. One thing was certain, I was not in danger of being robbed by anyone on that street. The policeman was right; the hotel manager welcomed me with no fear of being duped by a con man with a story as wild as mine. He consoled me and made sure that there was a hot bath drawn for me in the men's locker room, where I found soft white towels and a pile of clean gauze and tape to cover my wounds. It seems that just the mention of the local policeman's name and the fact that I knew Samuel on a first name basis was enough for him to accept me as family.

After my hot bath, there was a wonderful meal in the bar, where I was given an open tab, and I wondered if there had ever been more trusting people on this planet. Though I looked the part of a penniless beggar, these people treated me with respect and made this stranger feel very welcome. I suppose I might have been too bold to be disbelieved, but believe me they did. A combination of my prayers and great good fortune had carried me far, and in every way, this adventure was better than anything I could have ever planned. An angle or the Good Lord himself had done a wonderful job keeping an eye on me. Something had guided that conductor to my aid just before the divining moment had finished my days. I had much life to live yet, and this would be a great adventure story to tell my grandchildren. Truly I felt that my life was new.

But this adventure was not over by a long shot. My beloved boat was still out on that Great Lake, sitting alone on the cold, hard, rocky bottom, and I was determined to fetch her. It was the fall of the year, it was true, but the air was still warm, and the sun was still somewhat high in the sky, so I felt sure I could muster some sort of a rescue effort. Leaving this place and returning home without my boat was contrary to everything I had known. I would rather have tried to save her and failed than to not have tried at all. Getting that boat off the bottom had become my new obsession, and there was still time to get the job done before she would be lost forever.

9

THE NEXT MORNING, I sent my wife a long overdue telegram and informed her that I had indeed been lost, but now I was found. I also informed her of my urgent need for money and asked her to please forward some to the Western Union office from which the telegram had been sent. Then she should have a note of credit from our bank back home sent to the Sault Ste. Marie Bank and Trust Company, across the river in Michigan, where I would open an account. With words of love, I sent the telegram on its way, collect.

The policeman from the train station found me at the telegraph office and had me sign a simple statement which would allow me to stay in his country until my business was concluded, said business, of course, be the retrieval of my beautiful sailboat. He also wrote down a short statement pertaining to my skirmish with the fellow named La Chance, which I signed. Anything I could do to help keep that fiend behind bars was okay with me. He turned less official for a moment and put his hand on my shoulder. "You are lucky indeed not to have been killed by that creature. He has no regard for life, and no one knows how many men he may have killed. I myself have been on the alert for that man for over two years. He has been a fugitive living in the wild all that time."

We talked some more, and he listened intently while I told my story. I told him everything that led up to now and how I hoped to mount a rescue effort on my beloved boat. As a member of the revered order of the Royal Canadian Mounted Police, he told me he was not disposed to name any particular firm or person that could help in the retrieval of my boat. But it just so happened that he did have an uncle in the business of salvage, with a very strong steam-powered tug and a barge, who might be able to recommend someone who could help me. I was very grateful for the suggestion.

The salvage man in question was named Farley Smith, and upon making his acquaintance, I found him to be a burly grouch of a man. When I introduced myself to him, he stood with his arms folded and said nothing. After a pause of great length, I continued by informing him that I needed his service for a salvage job. Wordless, he listened until I had outlined the whereabouts of my vessel and its condition, whereupon he answered me, out the side of his mouth, "Next spring."

"Spring? That will not do. There will be nothing left by then. I need it done now," said I.

"Won't leave the dock this time of year, mister" was his reply.

I realized this man would be a hard sell, but I could see his equipment was up to the task, and time was of the essence.

"One thousand American dollars if we go now."

Suddenly a smile that I felt sure he would not have been capable of burst from his face as he forced out a question, "Why didn't you say you needed to go now? Would that be paid in cash?"

"Yep," I said in reply.

"Well then, I believe you have got yourself a salvage company, sir." He almost wrenched my arm from its socket, he shook my hand so hard. The grin on his face stayed there for days to come, and from then on, he found no trouble with conversation. It took only two days for me to come to legal and financial agreements with the Smith Salvage & Towing Company. By the end of those days, I had new clothes, a new disposition, and thanks to my wife, plenty of money to make things happen with. Down at the local barbershop, where I treated myself to a haircut and shave, I listened to stories about the great Captain Smith and his brave crew, setting out in a horrible gale to save a lake freighter from foundering. I was relieved to hear that this crew went out when others refused to go. Differentiating between brave and stupid didn't enter my mind at that point.

On the second day of preparation with the salvage company, I had received a letter from my dear Emma, and her words filled me with longing for home again. I made a resolution to never again leave her home alone, and if it was her wish, I would bring her with me on my next adventure, hopefully on *Nattily Ann*. Giving up the sea for a life on the shore was not so foreign to my thoughts these days, but I was sure that Emma would enjoy the occasional weekend out. My weakness for adventure had postponed by many years the expression of the devotion I so dearly owed my wife. Nevertheless, the thought of retrieving my beloved boat gave me great comfort and excited anticipation.

I spent seven restless nights in the Frankfort Hotel, and though the room was clean, bright, and airy, I felt confined and closed in. My emotions bounced between pure elation for my gift of new life and my burning desire to save my boat. The thought of tucking my tail and accepting a defeat at the hands of the sea burned me like a slow flame of harsh judgment. Taking the train back east would have surely been the worst thing I could think of that could befall me. *Nattily Ann* must be saved!

Farley's boat was a sixty-five-foot oil-fired steam tug and a thing of beauty indeed. My first sight of her told me of her great strength, and she was built out of black iron, which gave her a look of invincibility. Her bow stood tall with the name *Francine Smith* painted on each rail where the bow sheered to amidships, and then the rail rose beautifully to the round, wide stern. There was a large wooden cabin on deck, and the pilothouse rose up in front of the cabin, just before a very tall smoke stack with the letter S embossed on it. Below deck forward were the crew's quarters that slept four men, and there was nothing else below but a large engine room and boiler aft of the pilothouse.

I was given a small cabin with two bunks in it and just enough room to sit on a cabinet and take my shoes off. It did have a large porthole though, which I promptly opened in hopes of expelling some stale air. The air had accumulated inside that cell for a very long time, I was sure. It was one of two sleeping quarters at the stern end of the main cabin, with their substantial wooden doors opening aft.

In the main cabin, there was a good-sized eating area and a surprisingly clean galley. Captain Smith had a cabin forward of the ship's galley, and from what I could see, it seemed to be very comfortably appointed. Opposite the captain's cabin was a nice head and shower arrangement, providing plenty of hot steam heated water for long showers, if that was your wish. All in all, the tug may as well have been a boarding house afloat.

I was struck with the detail in the woodwork throughout the little ship. The Defoe Shipbuilding Company in Bay City, Michigan, had built the tug in 1927. The detail to which they had gone to putting the interior together reflected an expensive yacht instead of a common working vessel. Even the companionway steps into the engine room were made of mahogany, and Smith's crew had kept the varnish work up in fine order. The *Francine Smith* was a very fine little ship.

My assessment was that Farley Smith didn't possess the look of a tugboat captain. He looked more the part of a deckhand. It appeared, based on the good condition of the tug and the size of his home on shore, that he might have been well off. But to look at him, you would see an overfed, unwashed lout of a man, with his shirt hanging out and his shoes untied. His wife, Darlene, seemed very much the opposite though. Slight in stature and quite neat in appearance, she was a wonderful hostess at the lunch and social which they had invited me to, where we hashed out some pertinent details. Uncouth and sometimes brash, Smith gave one the feeling he might be somehow mentally handicapped, but once I had witnessed his handling of the tug, any doubts of his skill as a shrewd and capable boatman disappeared immediately.

In my almost forty years of seamanship, I had encountered many characters. People who live and work on the sea have a particular way about them, and I, for one, can spot them a mile away. This man Farley was a crossbreed though. He seemed to me to be half farmer and half sea captain. He was one of those men who knew his business all right, but there was no salt in his blood. So I thought. I was wrong.

A seventy-foot barge named *Sandy Island* was brought up along the port side of the *Francine Smith* and made fast. It was made of heavy wood timbers and had the traditional square slopping bow and stern, with high sides to accommodate loads of pulpwood, lumber, coal, or whatever. It was emptied of everything but lifting straps and some stout timbers, to act as shoring for *Nattily Ann* if the barge's small crane could lift her. Captain Smith (as I found he liked to be called) tried his best to alleviate my fears that the crane was too small by assuring me it had more strength than looks.

The crew was already sleeping on board, but Captain Smith and I slept ashore the night before leaving. We met that evening at the hotel pub, where he tutored me in his well-honed art of choosing a fine beer. The method for finding this beer required one to test two or three of the local brews before settling for imported Stout from England. The only way to truly get the taste was to drink a glass in one swallow, at least that was what he would do. Being a modest drinker myself, I listened and observed in case it would be necessary for me to engage in a search for a good beer sometime in the future. Smith's ability to stand and converse in decipherable sentences after hours of consumption struck nothing less than awe in me, for I myself witnessed at least two gallons of beer pour over the man's lips.

A handsome group of townsfolk gathered around the hearty-voiced man who was to be my captain. He definitely commanded an audience. It became apparent to me that there was much respect given to this man, and I was sure it wasn't just because of his generosity at the taps. I was accepted, but only on the fringe, although I was included in the conversations. One thing I found was that these people liked to laugh. I was sure he wouldn't think an early departure would be wise.

Slumber was at premium that night. Though my bed had been comfortable and the room quiet, I tossed in and out of sleep with pangs of anxiety stabbing at me, until I gave up trying as the first signs of light came sneaking over the horizon. I stuffed my loose belongings in my bag and walked the short distance to the docks. I was greatly surprised to see Captain Smith had already fired up the boiler, and the ship was alive with lights and activity. He was checking and securing the last of the lines holding the barge fast to the tug. He looked up at me with big sparkling eyes and asked how I was feeling with a wink that might have indicated the drinking bout was our own little secret.

While absentmindedly stowing my gear, a map of our activities was being laid out in my mind. I caught a quick glimpse of the stern of the barge through my port-side porthole. We would breast-tow the barge to open water and then let her go to be towed along behind us. Two hundred feet of one-and-a-quarter-inch hemp rope was coiled on the stern deck, ready to take up the strain as the barge was cast off to fall behind for the tow. A clear vision of *Nattily Ann* sitting inside the hold of this stout barge brought a warm feeling over my being.

The rushing sound of steam bursting from a relief valve brought me out on deck to see where it had come from. I almost bumped into Smith as he was rounding the cabin to get me. He informed me all was ready, and with my permission, we were off. He put his big hand on my back and walked me forward to the pilothouse and through the small oak door. It was dawning clear, and the barometer was high and steady. The east was bright and cloudless, and the west was clear as far as one could see. The temperature was about forty-five, which I believe to be high for that time of year in those latitudes. Standing in Smith's pilothouse, I looked at the gauges and valves needed to keep control of the little ship. The windows all around the cabin gave good view of about 275 degrees, and they were large, with each one having its own large electric fan to keep the fog and moisture off it.

Smith opened the cabin door and secured it wide. He stuck his head out and shouted for the lines to be cleared. Then he stepped to the ship's wheel and gave it a great spin to port and shouted "Steering left!" as any good helmsman would do. Then he reached down and slowly opened a valve, watching the gauge next to it. Steam was unleashed by that valve, and I saw the little ball in the gauge rise until Smith was happy with what he saw. Then he reached for a long bronze lever sticking up from the cabin floor and shoved it forward. This, I assumed, engaged the shaft, because I felt some movement when he did so.

Steam is a wonderful power as the turn of the wheel slapping water behind the boat can be heard over the sound of the pistons opening and closing their throats in turn. First one throat opens as the piston rises, and then it closes. Then the steam rushes in to silently push the piston down, and then the other piston repeats the effort, and so on, turning the crank that connects to the large bronze propeller. I was taken by surprise at the silent pull I felt on my body when the tug plowed forward from its berth. The barge obediently followed along by our side, after some stretching and bumping had been performed.

About an hour passed with the crew still stowing things here and there. There were four deckhands besides the captain and myself. Hans, who was the oldest member, a slight gray-bearded man at about seventy years, took the helm soon after we entered the St. Marys River. James and Raymond, both in their middle twenties, seemed to do most of the work, handling lines and securing every loose object to be found. Daniel Everit, with bright-red hair and a face to match, who was about sixty years old, was the engineer. His job was to make sure the engine and boiler were working perfectly. I met each one of the crew and shook their hands, all of them looking me straight in the eye. Seeing a smile on each of their faces, I felt quite confident I had made the right choice in picking this company. Never did I feel

I was a wealthy stranger in their midst. My immediate assessment would be greatly reinforced within the next so many days.

After we were well underway, Captain Smith wrapped his big arm around my neck as if to give me a bear hug, and swung me around to the cabin door. "Let's get some coffee in us" was his jocular suggestion. Out of the pilothouse to the next door aft, he bounced that door open with one shove of his big hand. I was shocked to see that there was a woman, dressed in bib overalls like a man, standing at the table. I thought of the woman back at Whitefish Point, but this woman was not nearly so large. She was bent over a table, wiping it down while holding salt and pepper shakers aloft. It struck me how spotless this mess hall really was.

"This is Mrs. Everit, Mr. Murphy. She is our cook and a damn good one at that."

I shook her hand and was taken aback by her strength and forwardness when she grabbed my hand in midflight as I reached toward hers. She greeted me with a distinct British accent, which I found very charming as I grew to know her. I was later to find out that even if she wasn't Daniel's wife, her prowess as a cook made her a coveted member of the crew. Every manner of gastronomic endeavor that was known to man had this woman beloved by all who knew her. Even lima beans had the taste of heaven, and yams were more like dessert than a side dish. It was no wonder Captain Smith spent so much time at sea. Never had I been fed so well, and never would I be fed like that again.

The good captain and I enjoyed a cup of Mrs. Everit's strong coffee as the tug left the bounds of land behind. The coffee was a brand that I was not familiar with. It was delightfully strong and tasted good. I suppose that, owing to my lack of culinary knowledge, my coffee would be quite insufficient for this crew. As we sat, I could feel the roll of the sea underneath us for the first time in a while, and it felt wonderful. It had been months since I had been to sea, and that might have been the longest time I had ever spent away from it.

We plowed through moderate seas in much the same path that I had driven only a little over two months ago. Our route would take us on a tack out into the big lake in order to avoid the rolling swells that were coming from the west-northwest. I had hoped to reach Montreal Island before nightfall and begin the salvage on the next morning, but as the month of November would have it, the wind picked up, and our progress was slowed considerably. By 4:30 p.m., we had made half the progress I had hoped for. The sky darkened with thick murky clouds, and the wind had risen to just short of a gale. As I looked over the horizon in hopes of finding a break, I was reminded of the strength this lake could show if she had a mind to. A feeling of foreboding came over me that could not be ignored.

By eight thirty that evening we were still on the same course, with the captain slowing to steerage out of fear of losing the tow. The tug rose and fell with ease. As the waves grew toward giant proportions, I began to voice some concerns to Captain Smith, but he simply looked at me and said, "This old girl can take it all right. Just pray she don't turn to the east." The barge was taking a hell of a pounding as the light of the ship's big search lamp told us. The full two hundred feet of hemp rope would sink into the water then, with a terrible jerk, leap up out from the water and snap taut with water spraying away from it in every direction. The barge's bow would sink out of sight behind a wave and then rise to a point where her bottom under the bow was in clear view. There was talk of adding another hundred feet of line, but even if we backed the tug down, the wind would carry the barge away faster than we could get the job done. Captain Smith did not want to lose his prized barge, so the decision was made to proceed as slowly as possible.

We each took turns at the helm, with the exception of Mrs. Everit. We would make a run for Montreal Island when it was safe to do so, which would turn out to be one extra day steering into that awful wind. The wind never did subside. Instead, it turned to the north and then to the northeast, giving us the first chance to close in on our target. That was good. What was bad was that the temperature had dropped below freezing, ice on the tug was becoming a problem, and the sea became confused because of the back winds.

Cloud-covered sunlight fell to the darkness on the second day, and little had changed. Each man was given a hammer or an axe to chip away at the buildup of ice that was gathering on any surface that caught the freezing wet wind. Neglect of this task would cause the weight of the ship to shift to weight above the water line, which, in the worst of circumstances, could cause the boat to capsize. The work was exhausting, and rest was at a premium. I knew that the chances of us having a clear run to Montreal Island would be slight, but I had not thought of the effect that ice has on a ship, and for the first time, I was less than enthusiastic about this endeavor. I felt badly that the crew had to work so hard to simply forage straight into the wind. It was cold, and the cold saps energy rapidly.

The old wheelman, Hans, stayed at the helm for hours at a time. When he was relieved, he would go out into the blow and chip as hard as any of us. I was ashamed to find my bunk by walking past him hard at work chipping ice off the stack. Was his dedication to work driven by fear, or was this man built of some human iron with an endless supply of energy? I have no memory of him sleeping or, for that matter, ever sitting down.

A couple of hours of sleep were not enough, but that was as much as any of us ever got at one time. Most of the time when I was woken, I felt worse than when I went to sleep. I remembered that it was sleep that had gotten me here in the first place, but life without sleep is no life at all. I struggled through that second night, beginning to wonder if this salvage was such a good idea at all.

Mrs. Everit would wake each of us for our watch, and she was the only one who never showed the lack of sleep in her face. As pleasant as she was, with her soothing "good morning," she never made me feel better about getting up. Everyone was suffering symptoms of delirium, and that would make for carelessness. It had only been two days at sea, and the cold was setting into the bones. I feared much more of this routine would cause a revolt. We were already out here, fighting tiredness and the elements, but bad idea or not, we were here, so the salvage had to be done.

At dawn on the second morning, Captain Smith pulled me into the pilothouse and sat me down to inform me that he felt that we should abandon the project. What had promised to be an easy recovery was now becoming a hazardous expedition. I rejected his call and found him to be of sound resolve. Tired and on the brink of exhaustion, I pleaded with him. We had come this far, and I was sure we could find shelter in the lee of Montreal Island, but he had made up his mind. He was sure that if the wind increased any more, or if the temperature dropped any lower, we were running the risk of losing a crew member, or worse, capsizing the tug and losing all. Forty-eight hours of pounding into that sea had taken its toll. Then I foolishly made another offer, either out of pride or just plain foolhardiness. Without thinking, I offered a bonus fee for the extra days, which seemed to change Smith's mood almost instantaneously. Looking back, I realize my mind was addled at that point and that it was a dangerous offer. Smith was right; we should have quit, but I was of unreasonable resolve.

He pondered my addendum to the contract for a while, and there and then we agreed I would pay an additional two hundred and fifty dollars per day and that I would throw a party for the whole town if we successfully returned home with my boat. The party idea was mine, and thinking about it now, I really somehow didn't believe I would be throwing that party.

After he conferred with the crew, who seemed reluctant to pass up the extra cash as well, he gave me a shake of the hand and informed me that we had struck another deal and that the salvage was back on track. He did reserve the right to call the whole thing off though if he felt we were in any more danger than we already were. I agreed; it was the right thing to do. I went away from that meeting feeling good about our future prospects.

Our course would put us in the lee of Montreal Island sometime after sunrise next, and that knowledge seemed to change the tenor of our plight. We drifted into a routine, with everyone taking a watch on the helm then giving the deck a sweep, cracking ice wherever it might be a potential problem. Lake water would spray over the bow and turn to ice or slush in the air before it hit the windshield. Snow formed in clouds like smoke rolling past the pilothouse doors, sticking to the windows, and someone would have to go outside and scrape the glass clear while standing on the freezing-cold deck, hanging on with all they had.

I was sitting in the pilothouse, warming my bottom on the radiator seat with Captain Smith steering, silently and mindlessly gazing into the white inferno, when the cabin door suddenly flew open with a bang. A howl of wind and snow circled into our previously peaceful sanctuary followed by one of the younger deckhands, which one I do not remember.

"Captain! You need to see this!" was his cry. "I think the barge is sinking!"

Smith beckoned me to grab the wheel and bolted through the door. I craned my neck around the door but could see nothing but the loom of the great searchlight. My curiosity caused me to lash the wheel and venture out to a point where I could see what was going on. There in the snow-clouded distance, dragging low in the water, was half of what used to be our tow. It appeared to be down by the stern and not responding well to the swells that were being thrust upon it. I knew something must be done quickly or she would be lost, and thus the salvage, but in this sea, what could possibly be done?

I held our course, reducing the boat's speed to the point where we could just hold her head into the pounding seas, waiting for the captain to return with orders. After what seemed an eternity, he burst into the cabin and asked me to go aft and help with the retrieval of the towline from the barge. Without knowing what it was he actually wanted, I pulled on my life vest and slid and pulled my way aft. No sooner had I left the pilothouse than I felt the tug turn broadside to the uncomfortably large swells. I arrived on the fantail just in time to grab the ice-encrusted line and heave it in along with the rest of the crew, including the impeccable Mrs. Everit. My bare hands stung at the freezing cold line's touch. We were drifting down toward the barge, which was wallowing in the beam of the searchlight. Hans was doing his best to stay focused. As a wave would throw us a little closer to the barge, we would all bump into each other, grab anything to stabilize our efforts, and tug on the stiff, freezing-cold line with everything we had in us. What we would do when we got to it was anyone's guess, but I felt sure Captain Smith had a plan.

After what seemed like forever, we had drifted down and were within spitting distance to the barge, and I could see that she was in real danger of going down. She was almost totally encrusted with ice and rolling lazily, allowing the waves to pour over her sides and bow. One time the bow rose so high over a wave that it looked to all that the barge was going to slip right under the water. She recovered but only by good luck. We all stood there looking, wondering what was next, when Everit went forward and, after a short time, came back with orders. The young seamen were ordered to tie all fenders along the port side, and the rest of us were instructed to fasten mooring lines to the cleats that were welded all along the port side of the tug. I can't help but remember Everit yelling, with his hands cupped like a megaphone, "For God's sake, be careful!"

These allotted tasks were all done with great difficulty because every movement would find the deck descending or ascending at us in either a forward or a backward motion, and always thrusting from side to side. There was no way to anticipate what would be coming next, so there were many trips to the deck, cracking elbows or wrists in an effort to break the fall. I felt unsure of where I was at any particular time, and dizziness came over me as if I were on some demonic carnival ride.

Then it happened. The most fearsome words a person could hear, the call, "*Man overboard!*" My head snapped around to see James shouting aft into the cold churning froth with his hands cupped around his mouth, yelling, "Raymond! Raymond!"

I leaped over a coil of line and staggered to his side only to see a glimpse of Raymond's orange life vest in the loom of the searchlight. Looking around to see if there might be a smaller line that could be thrown to him, I saw nothing. I scrambled up a ladder to the top of the main cabin, where Hans was running the searchlight. There was a life ring there with a long line attached to it, but when I grabbed it to lift it from its perch, I found it to be frozen in its place. There was no way it was going to come loose, and even if it did, the line was a solid mass of ice and thus useless.

Hans must have thought I was there to relieve him because he almost instantly let go of the light and climbed down the ladder, leaving me there alone. I grabbed the light, whose beam had fallen to the deck, and spun it over to aim it on Raymond again. Raymond was floating deep in the water with his hands flailing in what seemed to be a spastic effort to swim back toward the tug. I could see his head was bobbing from side to side like his neck was made of rubber. He did not look at all in control the way any twenty-year-old should, and I felt that he was impaired, as if he had hit his head or something when falling over the side.

Suddenly I could hear Captain Smith yelling orders from below me, and just as suddenly, James was cutting the barge towline with an ax. I could not hear what the captain said, but I knew that I should keep the light on Raymond. Looking back into the illumination of the water, the absence of Raymond in the light took my breath away. I swung the lamp first to the right and. after seeing nothing, swung it to the left. Still nothing. I enlarged the search to a circle pattern. When no sign of Raymond was seen, I enlarged the pattern even further. My heart pounded loudly through my ears. I fought back tears of panic. I remember hearing myself shout out loud, "Please, God, don't let him die!" I had lost sight of him, and time was working against us.

Was there any way he could have sunk beneath the waves in the short time my attention was diverted? Surely not with a life vest on, and he was trying to swim back to the boat. I could see the others pointing at the water, and though they were all shouting at the same time, I could not hear what a single one of them was saying. How could I have lost him in such a short time? These thoughts frantically raced through my head. I felt the tug's power surge as the captain swung the boat around. He had the presence of mind to check the compass and turn the tug toward the direction Raymond was floating, being pushed helplessly away by the wind and waves.

I scrambled forward, swung down the ladder next to the smoke stack, and bolted into the pilothouse, where everyone else had assembled. As I pushed through the door, everyone but Smith looked at me with expressions that let me know they blamed me for this mess. The reason Smith didn't look at me was because he had his eyes on the sea and his hand on the wheelhouse searchlight. It was as silent as a tomb in that room, and not a breath was heard until James broke out with, "Where the hell is he?"

"We'll find him" was all that Smith said, and then there was silence again.

Smith looked at his pocket watch then back at the sea. "Everyone go forward and yell out for him. It has been ten minutes since he hit the water, and I don't think he'll have much left in him if we don't get him now."

I knew what he was saying was true. The water had to be close to freezing temperature, and a body would lose most of its heat fairly rapidly out there. I clumsily asked Captain Smith if he wanted me to stay and run the light for him, but he took his eyes off his duties just long enough to look into my eyes, right through the center of my soul, and quietly told me to go out with the rest. That look told me just where I stood. It was me who should be out in the freezing cold water. It was me who had put the whole crew in danger for some quest that seemed so important to me once but was pale and insignificant now.

Everyone was screaming Raymond's name in unison and then waiting for some kind of reply. I couldn't make myself yell his name out loud. All I could do at the time was listen above the howling wind and pray that something would be heard or seen that would make this thing turn out all right. I was horrified at the thought of losing a happy blond-headed blue-eyed boy who seemed to have no fear of anything, smiling and laughing, even with me, who would most likely be responsible for his death. I felt the weight of the world sitting on my shoulders. For a brief moment, I felt like throwing myself into the sea but realized that action would not do anything to redeem me in the least.

Then at the depth of my self-pity, as I hung my head while grasping onto that pitching rail, I saw Raymond almost beneath the tug's bow! He was floating on his back with a face as pale as death, but his eyes were open, and he was looking straight at me. I turned to the crew, who were all on the bow, and yelled with all my might, "*Over here!*"

With those words I found myself once again airborne, but this time I was falling toward the water, falling like a rock with no thought of how I got there. I had instinctively jumped overboard, knowing I would not lose sight of this boy again. I hit the water with such a force that all the breath left my body. There was a searing pain of cold that instantly forced my body to begin shivering all over. I fought my way through the pitch-black entombment to the surface and found myself looking at the big tug's hull passing close-by me at a speed that would soon leave me and the boy lost in that cold, dark water. For panic-stricken seconds, I saw no sign of Raymond, but as I swung around, my outstretched hand made solid contact with poor Raymond's face. Thank God he reacted with a groan. I heard another groan from his mouth as I grabbed him and pulled him close to my body. He was very cold and stiff and incapable of moving his limbs. There was blood on his face and a gash of considerable size right above his eyebrow. Sounds came from his lips, but there was nothing that resembled a word. I wrapped my legs and arms around him in hopes of transferring some of my body heat to him even though our life jackets were holding us apart. I tried to reassure him that he was safe, but there was serious doubt in my mind, even if we were pulled from the water in a timely fashion, that he would survive. Water filled my nostrils as we dipped under and then popped to the surface time and time again. Raymond had no power to anticipate when we would go under, so I took to covering his mouth with my hand to prevent his swallowing and choking more than he already had. At first he was in a panic when I did this, but then he realized just what I was up to and seemed to relax.

The sight of the big tug pulling up to windward of us brought me hope, but the voices and sights were nothing short of hazy and far away. I became aware that there was someone else in the water with us. I knew I had heard a splash and felt someone pull a rope sling over my rapidly stiffening body with great difficulty. I had already lost the ability to lift my arms, and whoever it was that had separated me from the boy had to do it for me. I didn't know at the time who it was, but I did know that this person was surely an angel.

It was James who had helped me. I didn't know that until I found myself in the boiler room shaking uncontrollably, sipping hot coffee handed to me by Mrs. Everit. Raymond had been put on a cot right next to the boiler and was wrapped in wool blankets, so he looked like he was in a cocoon. Mrs. Everit ran her long fingers over the boy's head to soothe him and assure him he was in the company of loved ones. I watched this wonderful woman caring for the boy, and for a moment I found a strong attraction to her. She was nurturing and caring to the point of a saint. I flushed, embarrassed at the thought of her beauty, until I realized that she reminded me of my dear wife, Emma, whom I missed now more than ever.

It was very warm in there, and Mrs. Everit assured me that Raymond would be all right. She went topside to help in the retrieval of the barge and left me alone to watch after that brave young man. Someone had already bandaged his head, and as I folded my blanket over his shivering body, he turned his head toward me and uttered the word "thanks."

I said nothing, just patted him on the shoulder. My attention had been drawn to the tremendous clatter on deck. I peered through a starboard porthole and saw that we had found the floundering barge and were almost pulled up alongside it. I was groggy, but I felt a duty to be of assistance in its retrieval, so I left Raymond, who was now sleeping like a child, and climbed up the stairs to the pilothouse, where I found Smith at the helm. He was busy maneuvering the tug to the barge and offered no resistance to my offer to go help on the deck. I gathered a dry life vest from the hanging locker and pulled a dry storm jacket out as well. I was cold and soaking wet, but what difference would it make in just a few moments. Much effort was needed to get these items on because I was almost spent. If I hadn't known better, I would have sworn that I was completely drunk, but drunk I was not. If it had meant my certain death to go out there, go I would have, in hopes of even slightly redeeming myself.

I struggled through the pilothouse door and went on deck, where I saw that we were almost touching the sinking barge. It had been almost an hour since we cut it loose, and it was now very low to the water, ice covered and totally at the mercy to the waves. If it had not been for its one lone coal-oil lantern on the aft deck, we never would have found it in that darkness.

Suddenly the crew jumped to task of saving the barge, like a swarm of ants attacking a fallen wasp. We were alongside of the stricken vessel, which we secured to the tug, and efforts were immediately underway to manually pump the water out with the two-man bilge pump protruding out from the barge's forward deck. Mrs. Everit was already on the barge deck and pumping hardily when I first noticed the contraption was even there. I felt helpless, like I was involved in some sort of game that I had no knowledge of and didn't know the rules. People were whirling all around me without me knowing what was going on. I was handed hoses and tarps and line as the men uncovered a pump with single-cylinder gasoline motor that stood on the aft deck. A line was wrapped around a pulley, and after a great pull, the motor was popping away and sucking water out of the barge within minutes. Water from the stricken barge was being sucked through a four-inch hose then deposited on the tug's aft deck in great gushes, spilling overboard into the lake at its own will. After stashing the tarp and line under the ladder, I climbed onto the ice-covered barge with much difficulty to assist Mrs. Everit in pumping until her husband relived her so she could go and attend to Raymond.

Occasionally a great wave would replenish most of the water we had just pumped out, but after an hour or so of banging and crashing and breaking and splicing of lines, the old ice-encrusted barge seemed to be coming out of danger. It was decided she had taken too much water over her bow and had actually begun to scoop the lake as she fell to meet each wave.

We were lucky Raymond had taken the time to check her out when he did. We were also lucky that Raymond was saved from drowning, or should I say that I was the lucky one. If he had been lost, I would never have forgiven myself. I could only imagine how much guilt I would have suffered if he had perished. He had slipped and cracked his head as he fell overboard while trying to save a salvage that, under the circumstances, did not warrant the dangers I had put these people into. Reflection made me realize that the power of my money to make things happen was not always good. I was ashamed how I had let things get out of hand by bribing these people to risk their lives. My power had relieved me of my sense of priorities, and I vowed then and there to endeavor to never let priorities be ignored again.

As I stood on the barge's frozen deck, alternately lifting then pushing down the handle that Everit was on the other end of, I found it hard to make eye contact with that good man. Sweat was finding its way out of my freezing body, and I could see that Everit was every bit as uncomfortable as myself, but to him, this was just what had to be done. His way of life gave him no time or reason to make up excuses. His life was as real as the ice-cold water that we were pulling out of the sinking barge's belly. I knew right then that I wasn't even half the man he was, and I felt ashamed for myself. These people had worked tirelessly for three days and still managed the strength to pull three frozen, water-soaked bodies onto the boat. Then they had reserve strength to retrieve the sinking barge, secure it, and pump it dry, while all the time they were wet, cold, and had no footing. Their freezing fingers were pushed into the water streaming from the sinking barge's bilge in order to warm them up so they could continue to do their work. Their strength was monumental, and I was but a whiff in the wind of their superhuman abilities.

10

THE WORK HAD more than occupied everyone's attention. Only the old helmsman, Hans, saw the island in the predawn light. He was aware that we were closing on Montreal Island. Smith had kept track of the vessel's every movement in spite of all the confusion, and the chart clearly showed our location. Smith had taken the wheel from Hans and actually pulled the tow into the lee of said island while everyone else was resting in the galley and not even aware that the island was even there. Without a word, Smith drove us into the shelter of the southwest corner of the island, where the sound of the anchor letting loose from its mooring was the first the rest of us knew of our landing. We hadn't even noticed that the motion of the tug had lessened and the banging and crashing had all but ceased.

When our work was done and every little thing was back in its proper place, we all met in the pilothouse, where Mrs. Everit filled our cups with steaming coffee. Meaningless chatter filled the air along with nervous laughter about what might have been a real disaster being averted through pure adrenaline and damned good luck. That freezing sea had been but a moment away from claiming one of us, and if things had turned for the worse, it might have been all of us at the bottom of the lake. Everyone there knew how close it had come but said nothing, skirting the real issue, as if there was a ghost sleeping below and not to be woken. I, for one, did not want to wake any memories at that moment.

Smith spoke clear and strong when he said we would sit in that spot and rest until we knew what Raymond's condition would be. If Raymond was stable and could last out the salvage, Smith's boat would be put over the side, and he, Everit, and I would row over to *Nattily Ann*'s position and assess the situation. If the weather cleared and the back sea dropped, we would go forward with the original plan and begin the salvage. We all agreed that four hours of sleep was needed to replenish our strength, and every one of us but Smith left for our bunks. Each of us checked in on a warming and peacefully sleeping Raymond before retiring ourselves. His color was back, and his body had stopped shivering. It looked as if he would be all right. I lingered with him for a bit while he slept with no knowledge of anyone's presence, and I thanked the Good Lord for that boy's safe return to the living.

Smith slept on the bench in the pilothouse with a blanket pulled over his enormous body. I know he slept with one eye buried in a pillow and the other open to the world around us. I was convinced that this man missed nothing. I had seen him stretch out on that bunk, which acted as a seat for the crew when not being slept on. The wheelman and everyone who would pass through the pilothouse would tiptoe and whisper not to wake him, but the very moment the ship's clock struck his watch, he would bounce up as if he were not sleeping at all.

My own sleep was punctuated with the sound of steam rattling out of a small iron radiator at the foot of my bunk, whose only function in creation was to keep me warm. One could just imagine the consummate sounds of snoring and steam hissing and mixing, filling the old iron hull of such a sturdy little ship.

It was 7:30 a.m. on a cold, blustery, sunless morning, and I was very tired. My eyelids closed like a pair of iron doors and shielded me from any light that might try to wake me. I pulled the old wool blanket around my neck to keep all the heat I had near me. I was still cold, and it was coming from deep inside me. At quarter to noon, I heard the sound of anchor chain being pulled through a hawser. I sat up and, for a moment, wondered where I was and how I had gotten there. Looking out of the port, I could see we were moving more to the north and closer to shore. I lay back down to wake a little more and gel my thoughts. Even though the old war surplus wool blanket that covered me was stiff and scratchy, it had provided unusual comfort to me. This morning I felt like staying in bed all day. I was wracked with exhaustion, and every muscle in my body was making its presence known. The old tug was quiet and comfortable, and I would have enjoyed a day off, but as I knew, "If wishes were horses, beggars would ride."

How could we get that barge into the small cove where my boat was lying? Would the little crane really lift such a heavily built boat? Was my boat even still intact? How did Raymond make it through the night? It was time to see what was afoot, so I dragged myself from bed, donned my pants, and reluctantly left my little cell of comfort. When I arrived at the pilothouse, Captain Smith had pulled the anchor up by himself, letting the rest of us sleep on. He was rounding the island into the back seas and looking for the cove I had marked on the map. We were about a mile and a half from the cove, but the seas were running too high to safely enter. Smith decided to drop the barge on an anchor and continue looking for the target, so I was sent amid ship, where I began the task of freeing the barge from the tug. After climbing onto the barge and letting its anchor go with most of its chain, I finished untying it and let it go. It took over ten minutes to coil and stow all the dock lines, and when that was done, I took a moment for myself.

That morning, the barge appeared to me to be alive, sitting higher in the water for some reason. I started to go forward but stopped and looked at it again. That was the first time I had seen just how big and fine she looked. There was something that caused me to think of it like a dog jumping in anticipation of a walk. I really imagined it was as anxious as I was to get started pulling *Nattily Ann* off the bottom. Things seemed to have settled, and I was beginning to feel the adventure of this whole thing. I was excited at the prospect of seeing my boat and actually retrieving it and taking it back to civilization and a new life. Just one more resurrection to be had on this trip.

Now free of the tow, we could poke in if need be and take soundings and look for underwater rocks that would impede our success. I went forward and stared diligently at the shoreline in hopes of spotting something familiar. My eyes strained to see something that looked even remotely familiar as we slowly and silently cruised along the rugged shoreline. Nothing stuck out in the way of a land-mark, and every rock looked pretty much like another. I slipped into the warmth of the pilothouse, where Smith and I shared idle talk and sipped something he had brewed that tasted almost like coffee. I wasn't sure where he got the water to make it, but I suspected that the bowl of dishwater might have been emptied to make it. It felt good looking out from the safety of the pilothouse at Montreal Island's somewhat unfriendly shoreline.

Scouring the coast for something familiar erased the anxiety that had haunted me from the time we left the dock. I thought how different this place had looked from one hundred feet above. Actually, aside from my excursion in the pram the morning after the ground-ing, this was the first glimpse I had had of this place. I went back out and strolled to the forward deck to look over the bow and search the landscape, mostly so Smith couldn't see the gremmies on my face every time I took a sip of his coffee-like gruel. Suddenly I caught sight of something standing up over the rocks. It was the mast of my boat, and then I recognized the beach where my tent frame was still standing. I looked back at the pilothouse and pointed it out. I must have looked like an excited child, jumping up and down with joy.

Smith turned the tug's bow toward the beach to poke in as far as the swelling water would let him. Iron or not, if the hull should ride a swell to meet a rock, it could cause great damage. Instead, Smith sized up the approach to the cove as I told him what I knew about it. He set his mind on an early arrival to this location the next morning. We hoped the wind and wave action would subside by then so we could safely enter and exit.

I stood there in the pilothouse with Smith, talking over the situation. Looking at the mast, when I felt someone behind me. As I turned to look, what did I see but a six-foot-tall Raymond looking over my shoulder, eating an apple, saying, "Is that your boat?"

Much to my surprise, here was the young man I thought would be incapable of even walking, standing in the pilothouse and making idle chatter. Raymond had woken Smith earlier that morning, and Smith had even fixed him a hot breakfast. Aside from a bandage over his right eye, the boy was showing no ill effects whatsoever from his misadventure, aside from some weakness in his knees and an insatiable hunger. Raymond was as hardy as ever and had little memory of the whole thing. I, on the other hand, was in total shock that he was alive, much less standing in the pilothouse asking me questions about my boat. The captain and his mate stood looking at my wreck, making plans as if nothing had happened, while I stood dumbfounded, wondering at my luck and Raymond's incredible resilience.

Smith's knowledge of the lake had caused his caution, but the barometer was telling the story. It was rising steadily, and finally the sun was peering out from what had been an unceasing cloud cover. As Smith backed away from our shallow intrusion, I fixed my eyes on my little boat. How things had changed in such a short time. There she sat, covered in ice-cold water, resting on that cold, hard, rocky bottom. She was covered with patches of ice, and ice was sticking to her hull all around. By the look of her, you would think she would not be worth the cost of the salvage. I knew that only my eyes could see the true value of our prize.

My little beach prison was filled with leaf litter, and my camp showed it was an abandoned, lonely place incapable of supporting life. Memories of the simple life on that beach, sharing my stories with that wonderful bird, carried me away. I realized that time had a simple splendor for me, and somehow I missed it. My emotions were so close to the surface at that moment that I excused myself and went to my cabin to finish my rest.

That night, our fabulous chef prepared a feast that could be judged well by anyone's standards, with a turkey and all the trimmings put on the table. Beer and wine appeared as if by magic, and the warmth of the evening never left me until morning. Conversation went round and round, with laughter being generously proportioned. Raymond was the unofficial guest of honor for what reason he did not know, but the rest of us of had no doubts at all. I stood at the end of the table and prepared to give a toast to my incredible crew, but as I looked into their faces, I saw the forgiveness in their natures. Instead of a toast to good friends, I asked that they would forgive my foolish desire to save something so dear to me, but never so dear as the life of one young man who, by the grace of God, was still here with us that evening. By the end of that memorable evening, I was enriched with newfound friendships plus stories enough to fill a book. In their simple way, they had forgiven me and let their anger at me go its own way. Life inside the old iron tug was as sweet to the taste as any I had experienced on shore.

My sleep that night would be that of a god. Though these people were in my hire, they treated me as a friend, maybe because I worked with them and suffered with them, but they had made me feel I was one of their own. For that I was truly grateful because I had learned that friendship is really the only treasure worth having.

0600, Monday, November 11: Efforts to salvage *Nattily Ann* are underway. The sky is clear and sea is calm. Barometer is at 29.98 and rising. Captain Smith has informed me that we will push the salvage barge into position on the beach next to the salvage and attempt an easy withdrawal from that position.

As I penciled this into my log, I sat back and counted the days *Nattily Ann* had been there on that cold bottom. This was the fifteenth week of the near demise of my little ship and fifteen weeks from what was almost the end of me. Now, with any luck, she would be off the bottom and headed home before dark. Fifteen weeks seemed like a shadow with nothing to grasp but wisps of memory of time spent in contemplation. Nothing physical was left to remind me of that time but beach remnants and the boat that got me there. My wonderful airship was but a memory, like the warming fires that heated all those October nights. The stars had not changed, and the air was still as easy to breathe as it had been. What time is this that ranges from stump to bump and all I have is memory?

With the barge looming large ahead in our vision, young James stood on its bow, giving hand signals as to speed and direction. We were close, and I felt my heart quicken as we rounded the large rock that had so mercifully given me shelter from the killing waves. The barge bumped and scraped something, but owing to it being deeper in the water than the tug, Smith punched the barge forward until the beach was rolling up under her prow right next to *Nattily Ann*.

This was not the first time the crew had done this type of thing, for within minutes, they had started the engine on the little crane and were dragging straps and chains forward toward the beach. As I had no instructions for my part in this work, I strolled forward to watch and lend a hand where needed. It was but a short time before I realized this crew had it well in hand. I jumped down off the barge and walked over the old campsite, picking up my snow-covered wallet with money still in it and some other belongings of no particular importance. I was puzzled that my flock of gulls with Rufus in charge was nowhere in sight. I wondered where he might have gone and how my old friend was faring. I felt sorrow that the one-legged companion who had meant so much to me in my seclusion would probably never be seen again. Thinking over events that had taken place on that sandy spit, something caught me by utter surprise. It was the sound of wood being chopped, and before I could figure out where and why, I witnessed *Nattily Ann*'s mast falling down like a tree in the forest. I bounded over to catch the Nordic-looking James, with ax in hand, ready to chop my standing rigging as well.

"Wait!" I yelled with my hands in the air waving frantically in case he could not hear me. "Let me do that!" I shouted as I tried to find a way onto the deck of what I was afraid would soon be my little pile of kindling. I could see the disappointment in James's face because he was obviously enjoying this task. His double-headed axe was raised, and with one eye on the target, I just barely interceded in time. Finding tools to loosen the standing rigging and getting on board took long enough that by the time I had started the task, Raymond was chest-deep in freezing water pulling straps around the stern of my stricken vessel. His teeth were chattering, and he was doing his best to keep his arms above the frigid soup when just as suddenly as you could slap a fly, he disappeared under the water to rise on the other side in water too deep to stand. He had a line in his mouth, which he handed up to me, and then he dog-paddled back to the beach, where he was met by Mrs. Everit, who wrapped him in a blanket. It was hard to choke back my laughter as he stood there shivering with a slight tint of blue on his face and lips. He looked so young and strangely comical, shaking there the way he was. His eyes met mine, and I felt a pang of appreciation for a young man who had no fear of work beyond the limit of pain and fear. Considering what he had just come through, it was a miracle he would even get into the water, much less freezing-cold water. The job must be done, and he had done it.

The strapping of the bow was easier and done mostly from the deck and cabin top. Once my rigging mess had been cleared and the felled mast secured in the barge, a large steel cradle-like frame was swung from the barge over to the beach where the straps fasten each end to a corner. The little crane then lifted them and swung over the boat at the same time. I made a leap from my boat to the beach only to miss the comfort of dryness by a mere foot. My balance was lost, and if it hadn't been for the hand of Mrs. Everit, I would have fallen backward and into the water. Raymond found this humorous, and then it was his turn to laugh.

The time had come, and I stood motionless as the straps drew taut. The crane was in the hands of Captain Smith as he shouted orders for a last appraisal. All nodded in the affirmative, and the crane began to pull. Loud black exhaust billowed out of its skyward pointed stack, but nothing seemed to move except the crane being pulled downward and forward. Smith realized the little boat was heavier than she looked, so he relaxed the strain and repositioned the lifting arm to a more upright position, which changed the angle of attack. This exercise was repeated and went on for a time until it was finally apparent something else must be tried. With all the straining and puffing, *Nattily Ann* had refused to move. The barge's long tow-line was run from the stern of the tug through a fairlead and over the water to my boat. The line was too thick to fit any of my cleats, so I was forced to splice a smaller line, which was generally regarded as a useless effort, but doubling the line made up the strength. The donkey winch on the stern of the tug was then started, and as the strain was taken, it seemed there was movement in *Nattily Ann*'s stern. The crane was tried again, and this time, with the tow from the stern and the lifting motion, *Nattily Ann* broke free from the bottom. There was a cheer ringing from the onlookers as I felt a rush of elation. Caution was Smith's stock in trade, so all efforts were ceased while we sized up the situation. *Nattily Ann*'s stern was off the bottom and had swung out to seaward.

Slowly the crane gave a slow turn toward the deep water with *Nattily Ann* inching along with it. Up a little and back a little, then up a little and back a little, until she was hanging clear of the bottom and being slowly relieved of her heavy load of water. Tons and tons of water flowed out from the cracks that the encounter with the rocks had put into her bottom. It took a breath-holding hour before my boat was completely out of the water and an additional hour to get her into the hold. The crew then banged and pushed timbers that hadn't been lost overboard in the barge's almost sinking into a makeshift cradle.

As this was being done, I knelt to see the damage that had been done by the rock or rocks we had hit. Checking her soggy moss-covered inside showed how bad it was, but there was no doubt in my mind she could be saved. Smith seemed to have a differing assessment. He only looked at me and shook his head as I stated my optimistic opinion about her condition.

I was a happy man. Though daylight shone through her hull and the cotton caulking was hanging down from between the planks, I could see that the job of rebuilding would not be that daunting. Standing inside what had once been my comfortable home, she seemed so foreign to me with the cold dampness and slime-covered wood. The whole scene repelled me away from what was once her oh-so-familiar cabin. She was as dead as dead could be right there, but even as I stood looking at her broken body, I knew life would be given back to her in the future. It was strange and foreign to be inside her hull, like I was intruding into some very private crypt. I did not go back in there again until she was well under repair. There in the barge's belly sat my once beautiful boat, but at that moment, I saw her as barren as a graveyard. An eerie sense that death was in her left me feeling uneasy and strangely afraid of her.

While still inside, I could feel the silent pull of the barge being extracted from the beach. Captain Smith was backing into the lake as the crew routinely went about stowing and coiling everything in sight. I made my way back to the tug and was informed that, because of the wonderfully calm sea, Smith had decided that we would push the tow ahead of us as long as it was possible to do so. Captain Smith estimated that under these conditions we could make over eight knots and that would get us home sometime after midnight. That thought was reassuring to me. The tug made a large sweeping turn and headed out into the open lake as I walked to the stern. My eyes stayed on the place that had been my home in exile for so long until it was well out of sight. As I did that, a thousand thoughts replayed through my mind.

There were many nights spent alone there in an exile that I had not wanted nor planned, but while there, I made a life of it. Life is strange when you think of how one man's fate can turn so easily. Life was in me, and I was sure that life would soon return to *Nattily Ann*. For that short period of time, there on the deck, I became aware of how tentative our stay on this planet really is. I could see myself standing alone on that cold beach, longing for rescue, had it not been for the inspiration of one little bird. How amazing it was that I was leaving a place that could have very well been my grave. Instead I had survived and found the good fortune to throw in with such a wonderful group of people who mustered the strength to help me fulfill my dream. I watched the sun fall over the horizon that evening, and the smell of the cold water churning up from the tug's prop filled my senses. The cold air was welcome because I could feel it, and it made me know I was alive. How close I had come to not being so was still fresh in my mind.

11

THE WEATHER COOPERATED, and with a slight breeze from the southwest, we made good time in moderate to light seas. Shortly after 10:00 p.m., we sighted Whitefish Point light. It took a little over two hours' push until we entered the river, and twenty minutes later we were tied to Smith Salvage Company's dock, just as Smith had predicted. It wasn't long before all aboard but Smith and I had disappeared into the night. Smith wished me a good evening and apologized for not inviting me out for a nightcap, but it was late, and he was wanting to see his woman. I watched Smith walk up the dock and onto the road and thought of his late-night meeting with his wife. How nice it would be if I could only see my dear Emma and feel the love that she had always been so good at sharing with me. She never had a thought for herself that I could remember; instead she was always doing and caring for me. She had reared two daughters and never raised her voice to one of them. Instead her manner was to softly cajole each of us to her way of thinking. I am sure a gentler soul had never lived on this earth. My thoughts of her were deep, and there was no awareness that I was standing alone on that hard, chilly deck until I was jolted from those thoughts by the sound of a voice.

"Shotty? Is that you?" came a voice from the air.

I looked around to see who was calling after me when I spotted a figure standing alone on the quay. The light over the office door was dim, but I could see a figure of a woman standing there. "Yes, it is. I am Shotty Murphy" was my reply to what seemed an unfamiliar voice.

"Shotty! It's me, Emma!"

I could hardly believe my ears! The unfamiliar voice was that of my wife! I scrambled over the rail and almost tripped over myself as I ran toward her. Her arms were outstretched as I rounded the ramp to the quay and jumped over to her, almost knocking her down with the force of my embrace. What luck had brought this woman to me?

"Where did you come from? How did you get here? I have missed you so much!" Words were flowing nonstop from my mouth. It must have been a minute before she found a hole in this stream of words to speak into.

"I arrived just this morning by train. The trip was not easy, you know. This place is in the middle of nowhere! I saw your tug lights from my hotel window." Then she broke into uproarious laughter, as did I. We held each other in that very spot for what seemed like hours. If we had disappeared from the planet at that very moment, it would have been the happiest moment of our lives together. What greater happiness is there than true love?

We spent the night in her hotel room with the flicker of a fire in the fireplace glowing all over the room. We talked the night through, and she listened spellbound, as I told her every detail. I told her about a one-legged bird and a pack of ravenous dogs. I rapidly spit out the story of the great time I had with the hunting party. Sometime in the night I told her about a burly man who didn't seem to like me, leaving out the grizzly parts for her sake. She yelled "You what!" when I told her I had built an aircraft. "Tell me you didn't do that!" she blurted out as I followed with my finger raised up to my lip with a "Shhh."

We slept with our arms wrapped around each other and snuggled like young puppies sleeping in their mother's fold. At ten the next morning, we treated ourselves to a wonderful breakfast of hotcakes and blueberries in the hotel dining room. As we sipped coffee and tea, Captain Smith came in and sat with us. I introduced him to Emma, whereupon he deposited an uncharacteristically gentlemanly kiss to her hand, involving a slight bend at the waist. He then queried me on what to do with our cargo of soggy, rotting boat now that it was safe. Smith wanted to haul his barge out of the water for winter repair and storage. He also informed me that he had several barns on the waterfront, any one of which would accommodate my disheveled boat, if that was my wish. I informed him that I would consider our plans and discuss the subject with him later in the day. Emma and I hadn't had time to figure what our next move would be. I felt nothing at that moment but the desire to rest and spend time with my wife.

Smith had been told by his wife that a woman claiming to be my wife had arrived in his little town on the same day that we came back. Not much escapes the mouths and ears of small-town gossip, and this town was no exception. Mrs. Smith had been told by Mrs. Tipple, and she heard it from the hotel's janitor's wife, and so on. Actually, the stationmaster had figured it out when a lone woman asked for a ride to the hotel and if anyone might know the man named Shotty.

It was snowing fairly hard that day, and the air was sharp. Emma and I walked arm in arm to the dock, where she was introduced to the crew. Mrs. Everit was cleaning the galley when they met, and the two women hit it off almost immediately. I left them talking nonstop to each other and met with Smith to inform him that not only would I like to rent a shed from him, but I also wanted to hire craftsmen to repair my damaged beauty throughout the winter months. He was very happy to accommodate me and assured me winter work was scarce in his town, and it would be much appreciated. Sure enough, by the end of the day, *Nattily Ann* was winched into a fairly large storage shed, and work was already underway to renovate her. His crew started by putting a potbellied stove in the middle of the floor. Electric lights were installed within days, and holes were patched to keep out the winter winds. All in all, within a few days, the old shed turned into a warm, comfortable boat shop. I could almost smell the sawdust already.

As I had promised Smith in our negotiations, I threw a party for the whole darn town, and like I had done over the past months, Emma made many new friends at that party. We provided a gay luncheon, with tons of chicken and pork cooked over an open fire by the town's women, including the lady that had sent me on my way with that delicious chicken so many months before. The old fishermen who had been so helpful were also invited, and the crew of the *Francine Smith* was the guests of honor. I don't believe any man, woman, or child in town had missed that great Sunday luncheon. Though it was cold, with a prewinter wind lifting the tablecloths, everyone had a wonderful time. I observed Smith giving his famous beer-drinking lessons over one of the three barrels of beer we had provided for all to imbibe. The cost was enormous, and there was nothing left uneaten or drunk, as I was told the last to leave took the only remaining barrel of beer with them. The cost was nothing in return for the goodwill that was shared that day.

Emma was enjoying herself so much with her new friends and the simple life we were having in Sault Ste. Marie that when I suggested we stay in this community for the winter and help with the boat's repair, she was eager to accommodate my wishes. We rented a lovely little New England–style cottage near the hotel and moved in to an environment that felt almost as good as home. The cottage was within a short walk to the boat shed, and that little cottage gave Emma a feeling of home that makes any woman feel good. That winter we spent uncounted wonderful hours rekindling the feelings we found in our youth. Many a night I slept on the floor in front of the fireplace, wrapped tightly in my loving woman's arms.

Two carpenters and Everit were hired to repair my boat, plus old Hans to help keep the fire going and the place swept up. The carpenters, John Jokanen and his nephew, Harold, had many years of experience and came highly recommended. Everit was also taken on and found to be handy with a plane, but what is more, I just liked him. The boat shed took on a life of its own with many happy hours of genuine loving work. The hands that healed my boat were good hands, as anyone could see it. Again, I had chosen wisely.

Each and every day, some sort of progress took place. The boat took up the center of the shed floor, and a scaffold was built around it so the deck could be taken apart without standing on the boat. The bad planks were removed, and the rudder was unhitched from its mooring so the shaft could be taken out. Stripping her down to her bones gave her a very undignified look, and with everything taken off her, you couldn't tell if she was coming or going. She was in pretty poor shape, and a lot of time was spent thinking what would be the best way to make her whole again. Progress, though steady, was somewhat slowed by the onslaught of winter. Every day snow would have to be pushed away from the door just so we could get in. Firewood would have to be brought in, which often required several of the men because of the excessive cold and the fact that there was no insulation in the walls or ceiling.

Winter in those latitudes can be very harsh. I also learned that snow falls close to the lake without regard to one's ability to shovel it away. It seemed that snow fell every day, and by the end of January, there was nowhere left to put the stuff. I was forced to hire a man and his mules to cart it away in a wagon, to where I did not care. No sooner had he removed a load of snow, then the sky would open and give it all back again. In truth, the windows on the ground floor of our two-story cottage spent half the winter covered in snow. We didn't care though, because we had oil heat and lived in our little igloo in warmth and comfort.

I discovered that most people found it easier to move about on horseback in the winter. Automobiles were almost useless against the snowy onslaught. I relied on feet to go for groceries or stove oil once a week. Firewood was stacked dry in a shed next to the back door, so I burned much wood in the fireplace and wood-burning kitchen stove that winter.

Winters on the East Coast have very little snow, with the occasional storm followed by melting temperatures. Here there is something known as *lake effect snow*. Moisture from the lake lifts into the air and falls on land in the form of a light snow, so every morning you wake up to one inch of new snow. That is usually followed by a three-day northeaster that leaves up to as much as three feet. It took a while to get used to it.

One nice thing about this community was its library. Without it, we might have gone crazy. Emma must have read three books a week, and when she wasn't reading, she was meeting the women folk at the library for a social. Occasionally the women would ride the bus that crossed the bridge into America. There was a Walgreen's drugstore there that had a soda fountain. I think it was a favorite of theirs. Also there was a J. C. Penney's, where they could buy cloth for sewing and necessaries that were too expensive in Canada. I think they just needed to find things to keep themselves busy. For me, I had everything I needed within walking distance from home.

My kinship with Smith grew over the winter also. As I got to know him better, I grew to like him much. I was happy to find that not only was he an accomplished seaman, he had obtained a formal education and held a diploma in the letters. He started his working life as an instructor at a Canadian college teaching English. There he met the future Mrs. Smith, a student at his college, who was born and raised in this delightful community. After she graduated, he couldn't stand the separation, so he followed her to Sault Ste. Marie and took a job as a mate on a tug just to be near to her. As true love is wont to do, he asked for her hand in marriage and forsook his teaching career for a more exciting and better-paying job as first mate on a salvage tug. Like my grandfather, Smith had worked himself into a position where he bought out the old owner of the tug, and within a few years, he had built himself quite a reputation in the business.

I would sometimes wander into the hotel bar where he spent much of his idle time. There I would engage him in spirited conversations about things such as physics, astronomy, or whatever. He was an avid reader and kept up on international news, which I found to be most interesting. As he introduced me to his group of friends, I discovered he was a man who was able to conduct a conversation no matter who he was with. The uneducated men who worked at the coal and oil yard felt just as much at home with Smith as did the president of the local bank. When I look back on those times, Smith stands out the most. He was enormously popular and friendly for no other reason than that he was genuinely a good man. I never hesitated to take his suggestions as to the boat's repair or most other things for that matter.

It is strange to me that somehow this man had a paternal influence on me even though he was almost ten years my junior. Emma has kept in touch with the lovely Mrs. Smith for all these years, and I was greatly saddened and distressed to find out that the bigger-than-life Smith had succumbed to a bout of pneumonia. Another great influence had passed from my life. My memories of him are fine indeed.

I remember the time that Mr. Jokanen discovered that the blow to *Nattily Ann*'s keel was worse than previously thought. It would require about ten feet of timber to repair it, but I felt that might make her weaker than she was at birth. To replace the entire keel from stem to stern would take much more time and money, but I would not feel right doing less. Fortunately there was ample sawn lumber to choose from at the local sawmill. Finding the proper wood became a whole other project in itself. Smith, Emit, Hans, and I spent many hours shoveling snow off one pile of lumber after another at the saw mill, while the sawyer tried to remember just where those oak timbers were. I began to wonder if he had said oak timbers at all. Half a day was spent searching with no luck, so Smith went to work on him and pried his memory loose over a heavy bout with beer that evening. That next morning, a hurting and timid saw master took us to the snow-covered stack of oak that we needed. It took six men and the mule-drawn wagon to fetch it back to the shed. Smith confessed that the clever old man had found a way to get the snow off his piles without doing a lick of work. Smith always had a way with people and usually found the best way to get things done.

That part of the rebuild was the touchiest. It forced the hire of extra hands, and I was required to buy every wood clamp that was available in the two adjacent cities. The job was enormous. We used enough wood bracing in tying things together to heat the shed for a month after we finished that part of the work. We suspended *Nattily Ann* off the ground and removed her entire backbone and left absolutely no room for error. Only a handful of frames had to be replaced aside from the whole keel. Other than that, the boat was put back original. I inspected every inch of the operation and was well satisfied with the superb craftsmanship.

As the work progressed, there was the view of a boat with her framing exposed on the bottom side, some gray with age and some standing out bright and new. Each joint had a tight fit, and where there was a meeting of an old frame and the new wood of the keel, it made a fine picture of just how good the craftsmen really were. Even with steady work, we were only half done by the end of February. I figured that the boat would have to be out of the shed by at least the end of May in order to rig her properly so we could depart by the middle of June on our trip back home. I felt that we could leave sometime in July and still make it back in good weather, but I didn't want to push it. What was more, a leisurely pace would be more enjoyable for the two of us. Emma is very fond of sightseeing.

I made every effort not to seem anxious to the crew; they were working as hard as anyone could expect. Instead, I would do everything that was needed to hasten the project. I engaged myself in a mental game, trying to anticipate what they would need next to do their jobs. Sometimes Jokanen would turn around to find me handing him the saw that he was about to go looking for. That might have been somewhat obnoxious, but it was effective. Sometimes the men would look at me as if I were crazy or physic or something. I am sure they had to wonder what I was up to.

There was one character who used to stop at the shed and warm himself almost every day. He was a strange little man named Henry, who had a very unfortunate limp. Apparently he had fallen off a ship that was passing through the Canadian locks, and as a result, he had broken his leg badly. The leg healed poorly and caused him to walk with an aggravated gait, which would alternately lift and lower his body several inches every step. This was a very strange sight when you saw him coming. The men in the shop referred to him as "step and a half," but never would they say this to his face. No matter how hard I tried, I never got used to seeing this sight. The boys knew Henry when he sheepishly stuck his head through the door one day. He had a grin that was too large for his face and eyes that always sparkled for some reason. Emit told him to "come on in," and in he came, every day thereafter. After his fall, he had spent the better part of a year in the hospital, having been left behind by his England-bound freighter. He had no one of his own back in England, so he just stayed on in Canada, selling daily copies of the *Detroit Free Press* to keep himself alive. I finally agreed to a subscription, which turned out to be a good thing. Smith, who also subscribed, and I would review the stories often. Smith would pick out an article or editorial that he greatly enjoyed discussing with me. That paper got passed around during our coffee breaks and at lunchtime, but I would take it home every night and devour it before and after dinner. That was the first time I heard about that little freaky mouse they called Hitler. It was heart-wrenching to find out what was going on in Europe in those times. Sometimes I would think how safe and sound I felt just being in such a wonderful place. My wife and I were very fortunate not to be, by some fate, living in Europe instead of America.

Everything in America, or Canada for that matter, seemed to be going quite well for folks. The Great Depression was slowly receding, and people were going back to work. Aside from some violent labor strikes, North America was as strong and healthy as any country on the earth. I felt very sorry for the poor souls over in Europe. Oh, to have had a crystal ball back then!

Henry had a delightful British accent and would grace us with a little editorial each day. When someone would chide him and ask if what he was saying was true, he would put the paper down and lift his hands over his head, putting his fingertips together forming a steeple and say, "It's God's truth!"

It was Henry who inadvertently read a story from the Canadian section one day that caught my whole attention. "Lookie 'ere," he said. "Seems that bloke you wrestled with on the train has escaped from jail!" Holding the paper up toward me.

I took the paper, and sure enough, there was an article about how one Andre La Chance had overpowered two of the king's guards while they were attempting to transport him to the provincial prison. He had escaped, nearly killing one of the guards in doing so. There was a very large manhunt executed with no positive results. It was assumed he had fallen through the ice while crossing a river and drowned. Apparently a heavy snow forced the end of the search before finding a body. Somehow I found it hard to believe the story of falling through the ice, and I doubted that he was dead. For a brief moment I remembered the curse he had given me as they dragged the blackguard away.

That night I had a dream about La Chance. I dreamed that his menacing figure had crawled on the snow-covered ground and snuck into a bear's den, where he found a warm place to hide, while outside there were Mounties looking all around for him. Then in the dream, I saw him standing in smoky sunlit woods, eating that bear's flesh while wearing its hide over his back. I was so disgusted by this vision that I somehow made myself wake. I never told anyone about the dream, but I did think of it for a few days thereafter. It might have been a vision of the white bear hunter for all I knew. That dream unnerved me enough to make me think about my useless pistol. I asked Smith if he knew anyone who might know how to fix the old blaster. He told me of a farmer just north of town that built rifles and repaired firearms for a living. He lived alone and had no phone, so Smith volunteered to drive me to his home, which he did one Sunday morning after Smith had gotten out of church.

As we passed the edge of town, Smith was kind enough to recite the entirety of that day's sermon to me. I could see that he was still full of the Spirit, and he must have felt it was his duty to pass the sermon on to me, who, for all he knew, may have been nothing more than a common heathen. I believe the sermon was some study on a verse from Matthew, and at one point, when Smith was lost for a quote, he was shocked to find that I knew the quote by heart. Amongst many of Smith's attributes, his devotion to the Catholic faith was admirable.

Being constantly at sea as a youth gave me very few Sundays off. Notwithstanding, it was the goal of one of my captains to make sure that I became well-versed in the teachings of the Lord. Captain Carstarfin gave me my first Bible, and that tattered old Bible had been my only reading material for many years. I told Smith that whenever I was home, I would attend the Presbyterian Church my wife's family belonged to, and because I couldn't keep my mouth shut on praise and verse, they made me the Sunday school teacher. I could see Smith's lip turn slightly up when he found that I prayed in a Presbyterian Church, but I assumed that he just overlooked that point when he was in doubt of my power to reason on one or another subject. By the time Smith turned his rather impressive model B Ford roadster up the farmer's drive, it was I who was giving the sermon. I don't believe Smith had ever been so silent. Even as we opened the doors to get out, all he could do was stare at me in wonderment. I truly believe he was in shock. I felt good that I could impress the great Captain Smith.

The farmer, Mr. Becker, was a small, slightly bent-over man in his seventies. His face was like a storybook, telling of the endless years of hard work subduing the wilderness and building a farm. He seemed very surprised to have visitors, though he knew Smith. Smith had explained why we were there, and he seemed confused, though he invited us in right away. His house was full of family photos, mostly very old and somewhat creepy. At first the look of his home was that of a place, though full of the things of life, that was not lived in. I don't think anyone had sat in his dusty living room for many years. As he ushered us into the kitchen, I could see that my assessment was correct. It was more than obvious this man's entire existence was in this one room. He even had a cot in there with a pillow and blanket that made me sure that, aside from the trips to the outhouse, he never left this kitchen. There were stacks of papers and magazines and old boxes everywhere. There was hardly room for three people to stand. Right in the center of the room was a large white porcelain-topped table. On it was a rifle stock and barrel. I picked up the stock and inspected it to see some fine carving of deer and fowl mixed into a forest scene. The barrel was octagon shaped and looked longer than normal. He explained that he was building a .22 caliber squirrel gun for a neighbor's fourteen-year-old son. I was quite impressed. I felt I would like to own one of his guns myself.

I pulled out my .45 caliber Colt, which was tucked into my belt, and as I did so, there came a feeling of power I had not felt before. The weight of the pistol is substantial, and by nature, this weapon is very dangerous indeed. For a moment I felt that if there would be any malfeasance or interfering in my life again, the offender's life would surely be in jeopardy from the barrel of this gun.

Becker struggled as he put on an overcoat and took us out the back door to a little clapboard shed on the edge of his yard. There he had loads of gun parts and guns of all sorts hanging from his walls. He studied my gun, did some measuring, and surmised that he would have to rebore the barrel if it couldn't be replaced. Some time was spent going through drawers looking for a replacement barrel, which he couldn't find. He informed me it would cost me two dollars for the repair, which he said might exceed the value of the weapon, but I assured him it would be worth the cost to me. I thanked him, and we left.

As we walked back to Smith's car, I could not help but note the collection of old equipment this man had around his yard. Hay rakes and mowers and an old John Deere tractor that looked like it hadn't been moved in years. The barn was sound but neglected, and aside from a scraggly cat, I saw no other animals. What I was seeing was the death of something that had once been very much alive. One time this farm had people living and working hard and happy lives. I could imagine women and children about the place, for it would have taken many hands to run a place this size. These thoughts saddened me much. I felt sorry for that man in his lonely, declining years. I did take note. This scene reminded me of how fragile life could be. I thought of the piano in his living room and wondered who might have played it. There was a little mystery here, and my curiosity was up. I had a feeling that we should have stayed and made small talk with that man. I would have loved to hear his stories, for Smith and I might benefit from his experiences. I saw some medals on the mantel next to a picture of a man wearing a military uniform. Had he fought in the Great War, or was that a dead son? There was something I wanted to know about him, for some reason.

Smith must have been thinking along those lines also. The day was sunny, cold, and very clear. Our breath hung in the air like miniature clouds floating lazily away on light air. Few words were spoken, and nothing was said about what had just transpired. I was dropped off at my home but found myself subconsciously turning away from the house and walking to the boat shed. Though we worked every day but Sunday, I felt a slight melancholy and decided not to infect my wife with it. I knew that seeing my boat in her state of repair would cheer me up.

We would let the fire in the stove go out on Sundays, but I spent some time stoking one up anyway. Why is it, I asked myself, that one person's life is so abundant and others have so little to cherish? Fate or whatever it is, had given me the ability to live as free as anyone in the world. I had no practical experience with the word *no* and feared nothing that I could think of. As I stood there poking at the glowing flames, I regretted that I hadn't the power to make things right for others less fortunate than myself. Maybe it was the sermon, or maybe it was thoughts of mortality, I don't know, but this malaise lasted most of that day.

That night, before bed, Emma and I discussed what we could do to show our appreciation to these good people and possibly improve their lives. Nothing really came to mind aside from donating money to the library, but that might not have served the entire community. We were strangers in their community, and they had accepted us kindly. I was spreading some money around the community, but we felt some greater gesture would be nice. I discussed this idea with Smith, and he made a good suggestion.

The only bell in town was one that hung in the steeple of his church, but alas, it had cracked and been rendered useless. It was the only thing that reminded the people that it was Sunday and time to worship. It also served as a timepiece for the town, ringing the chimes of the hour from six in the morning to six at night when it would signal the evening Mass. At 6:00 a.m., it would ring once and then again every half hour until 11:30 a.m., when it rang eleven times. At noon, it rang only once. At 12:30 p.m. it would strike twice, and so on. Twelve strikes signaled 6:00 p.m.

Service bells were always rung on the quarter hour so as not to confuse the routine. At that time, the bell would ring constantly for one minute, which would give the parishioners no excuse for missing church if they were anywhere within earshot. From what I surmised, the bell was much missed, and everyone we asked would love to have it back. I took the precaution of asking as many people as I could. The grocery turned out to be a good place to query the townspeople. There was a strong cross-section of citizens going through there, and without exception, they were in favor of the bell returning. It sounded like we might have a good project afoot.

The parish priest agreed to let Smith and I survey the bell situation. He led us into the tower chamber and climbed the ladderlike stairway to the loft ahead of us, lifting his long robe, and in so doing, he exposed the fact that he was barefoot in the middle of winter! Father Gilmore apologized for the condition of the tower because of its long neglect. There were ample cobwebs and dust about, but it was easy to see the workings of the bell. There was a long rope attached to the pitman arm that would swing the bell. The rope fell down through holes in the three levels to the ground floor, where it would be pulled by the bell ringer.

Aside from the normal method of ringing the bell, there was a clocklike mechanism that, when wound up daily with its model T–like crank that stuck out its side, would strike the bell with a large brass hammer on the hour and half hour. Obviously the brass hammer was the culprit that had broken this beautiful one-ton brass bell. Someone had tried to repair the crack with a series of drilled holes and bolts, but it was apparent the repairs could not hold up to the hammer. I was told that the bell was not more than forty years old, but it had sat silent for at least five years. Smith strained to think just when the last he heard the bell ring was.

Father Gilmore, Smith, and I reasoned how big a job it would be to effect a repair. It was decided to get Micah Hayes, the mayor, and Gideon Pritchard, the owner of the town's only bank, involved. This would make the effort more like a town enterprise, and because I wanted my involvement to be anonymous, it would appear as if I was involved only as a consultant. Smith, Pritchard, and Hayes agreed to keep my name out of the scenario and shield me as much as possible so as not to make it look like I was grandstanding. Two hours later people were congratulating me on my effort to repair the bell!

The problem, as we saw it, was that the bell had been installed first, and the belfry was constructed around it, so it could be very expensive to take the bell down. This set my mind to work. The bell could only be repaired in the Detroit foundry, where it was built. Getting it there would be easy. Getting it to the ground would be a different story altogether. Once again I found myself at the old drawing board. It was nothing short of insane for me to get involved in another project at that time, but I felt sure the others would be capable taskmasters with me doing nothing more than writing the checks. That was a false assessment. From the time the scaffolding was erected, there were daily decisions that, for some reason, only I could make. It seemed there was no engineer to be found who could handle a job of this sort. It was too small for the big guys and too big for the small guys. Even Smith, who had a vast understanding of physics, felt unsure about this job.

Physics is a hobby of mine, but I have had no formal education in it. It seemed easy enough to design the gibbet that would swing the bell out from the tower, and removing the south wall of the tower offered only a little challenge, but my sizable crew and foreman seemed dumbfounded when given even the slightest challenge. Surprisingly it was Henry, the paperboy, who offered the most help. Without being asked to do so, he handed me a detailed sketch of a wood-framed gibbet that would swing the two-thousand-pound bell over the edge of the tower. It was a simple design, but the detail with which he drew it was impressive. The measurements and even the angles had been drawn in. There was quite a story on that one little scrap of paper. In addition, he pointed out to me the flaw in the scaffold construction. At his instruction, more bracing was installed midway up, and strapping was driven into the tower to hold the scaffold tight. I was impressed indeed. Old Henry, it turns out, was no ordinary seaman. He had been first mate before his fall and was a graduate of the British Naval Academy. What a boon! Henry took the load off my shoulders and, in the process, gained new stature in the eyes of Sault Ste. Marie.

Because there was no record of how the bell had been lifted fifty feet off the ground, we were on our own. As soon as Henry was given the position of engineer, I was consulted only occasionally. It took about a week of bumping into each other, but progress was steady from there on. Henry had decided to take the bell to the ground in three stages. It would be lowered from its perch to the first scaffold landing twenty feet below. This would require one hundred feet of rope and two sets of blocks, the top one having five pulleys and the lower having four. The process would be repeated until the bell was lowered to a truck bed for the ride to Detroit. The plan sounded good in theory, and it looked good on paper.

I would take my lunch break at the church and was entertained by the number of onlookers observing the work. There was a medieval pageantry that seemed to evolve around this noble effort. The crowd of onlookers, having little else to do in the winter, had begun building warming fires in garbage cans and brewing coffee and roasting all sorts of creatures on the mesh put over the cans. I had a suspicion that the only time the crew really worked was when I showed up on my lunch break.

Father Gilmore was extremely grateful to me, not for the bell project, but for giving him a chance to find some of his old parishioners standing about in the bell project audience. The young raven-haired cleric worked the crowd like a carnival pickpocket and shamed or cajoled the backsliders into returning to his services. His count was over twenty before the project was done, and for that, he assured me a special place in heaven. I was impressed by his youthful exuberance and devotion to his duties. Any human who devotes himself with such fervor is worthy of respect, I say. Especially this man, who had to suffer so greatly with the cold and poverty he had sworn to embrace. His duty was to serve the goals of the church, and he appeared to be doing so very well. Shepherding his human flock, like his brethren in the church, was the only life he would ever know.

One day while at work in the boat shed, I saw Smith's roadster pull up with Father Gilmore in the back seat. Smith came in and asked me to come along with them. It seemed that the old gunsmith had died, and Smith was taking the priest out to his place to give the old man last rites. Smith felt this would be the time to fetch my pistol, if I wanted it back at all. I pulled on my jacket and jumped into the car, saying hello to the priest, who simply nodded in recognition.

We pulled in the drive and saw a police car and a hearse there also. The hearse must have just arrived because they were in the process of opening the back door and removing a litter. Smith and the priest went up to the house, but I headed straight for the gun shed. I pushed the door open, hoping the officers would not notice what I was up to. I wanted to retrieve the gun without being questioned about it. I was not sure if it was legal for me to have the gun in Canada. At any rate, there in a box sitting on the bench was my gun. It was as clean as new, and I could see that the bullet had been dislodged. From all appearances, he had fixed it and cleaned it before putting the gun in the box. I rolled the chamber and looked down the barrel. Every bit of the gun looked sparkling new. The old-timer had done well. I looked around to see if I had been noticed, but everyone else was busy at the house. I shoved the gun into my belt, pushed two American dollar bills into the empty box, and left the shed. I had a feeling that I had done something wrong, and I was very stealthy as I went about hiding the gun under the front seat of the roadster. Then I sat there in the cold car and watched all the activity on the farmhouse porch.

It turned out that the mailman, who was passing by, had found the old-timer. He had noticed that Becker was sitting motionless on the front porch and had not waved as he usually did. The mailman stopped in his tracks, feeling that something might be wrong as it was well below freezing that morning. Backing up, he could see that Becker had died, apparently while trying to rest or fight off a heart attack or something. The old man's head was slumped down against his chest, and his hands were clenched tightly to his jacket. There he had frozen solidly in place and in time. The postman then drove to the next farm that had a phone and called for the constable to come out.

Gilmore had arrived too late for last rites but said a prayer over the old-timer anyway. He accompanied the stiff and bent body out to the hearse and waited with Smith by his side until the back doors were closed on what was nothing more than an old panel truck by its appearance. We then waited until the procession had left the driveway when Smith asked me somewhat in code, "Are we okay?"

I nodded my head, pointing blindly to the seat, and he nodded in affirmation. The priest looked bewildered. On the way back to town, Gilmore mused over the frailty of life. "Life is like a flickering candle. So fragile and only here for a short time. Then comes an ill wind to blow it out." He said this with a quiver in his voice that made me suspect he had recited this speech before. I was sad for the old farmer and hoped he was truly in a better place, but I was happy when Gilmore was dropped off first. I had my gun and good friends and good health, so Gilmore's little speech was soon forgotten. I went into my warm house and hugged my wife for a longer time than she was comfortable with.

The big day was at hand. Henry had made all the preparations to remove the bell and ship it off to Detroit on Tuesday, the nineteenth of February. The truck was hired, and Henry had scrounged up a few of the hotel bar boys to provide the extra weight he felt would be needed to handle the ropes while lowering the bell. I was on hand and was not totally convinced of their sobriety for this occasion. One thing for sure, these were big boys. There was easily close to a thousand pounds among them. It would be their job to let the rope slide through their leather-gloved hands as the bell was lowered down and, when necessary, lift it back up.

I watched as Henry gave them instructions to wrap the line once around a large iron cleat that had been attached to the tower wall especially for this maneuver. It seemed they were well-versed, and there they stood, waiting. Then Henry gave the order to pull the bell up slightly so it could be swung over the side of the tower. The rope men pulled, and the bell began to lighten. It was a good plan, and everything was going well as the tower crew removed the bracing and slowly pushed the bell out over the edge of the building. Then the trio was instructed to start lowering. The problem was that they had forgotten to wrap the rope around the cleat. It probably would not have mattered, but one of the boys remembered the mistake and took his hands off the line to wrap the end around said cleat.

This still didn't matter because there was plenty of purchase for two of them to handle the weight of the bell. Everything seemed under control until the second boy let loose of the line to grab the end of the rope behind his buddy who had absolutely no strain on the line at all. What happened next was pure comedy. The only boy who was holding the line found that the load was getting away from him. He wrapped the line around his hand and tightened his grip to stop the slipping, and with that he was lifted right off the ground. Upward he soared at an increasing speed, with his eyes as big as saucers, until he came to an abrupt stop a good seven feet off the ground.

The bell crashed into the first landing and miraculously stopped without breaking anything. For breathless moments as the dust cleared and people started breathing again, the boy hung there yelling like a schoolgirl in one continuous belch. Before he was through yelling, I had pushed a long ladder up against the building and underneath him. With soft, firm words, I tried to convince him to let go of the rope and grab the ladder, which he finally did. The poor boy was shaking like a leaf as he descended that ladder, and it was all I could do not to laugh out loud. His friends were not so controlled; they guffawed and laughed without shame. It took a good thirty minutes for that round red-faced boy to gather his composure, but by the time the bell was rerigged, he was up to the task once again.

It was very cold that day, and I remember seeing people's breath floating skyward as the crowd cheered when the bell finally landed on the truck. They began to break up, each in their own direction, before the truck had left for Detroit. It took almost a month for the factory to slowly heat the bell to the proper temperature and repair the crack, but by the time the bell returned in the spring, the crew was confident and ready to put it back. I remember still the beautiful sound that came from the bell as it rang out its first chime in over five years. Everyone in town rejoiced at the ringing that first day, and within weeks, the clang of the chime was as common as if it had never disappeared at all. At the commemoration service, Father Gilmore openly thanked Emma and myself for the gift, which was exactly what I did not want to happen.

Much to my surprise, the story of the bell repair had made it all the way to Detroit and into the newspaper. Someone had gotten a photo of me and written about the whole thing, flying boy and all, and even mentioned my name as "the wealthy benefactor." I suppose that in itself was all right, but unknown to me, there was a certain criminal who happened upon that article and recognized my picture. It was that loathsome article that was to set my life adrift once again.

12

S PRING DID COME, and with it a brand-new life for *Nattily Ann*. With a new mast and bottom, her new paint and sails, she was all but a brand-new vessel. The old engine, having been retrieved from the beach, was scrapped, and a new universal four-cylinder engine was put in her place. Launch was completed in late May of 1939, and for all I could see, she might have been the most beautiful boat ever to float. The boys had done their jobs well, and truth be known, she was better than new. My pride was once again peeking at the sight of her. It had been a long, long journey from that August storm to that moment she once again entered the water. She was ready for anything now, and I was sure of that.

Winter took its own good time leaving those regions that spring, and our progress was slowed to a crawl. Emma and I reluctantly set about preparing to leave the little cottage and these wonderful people. I think that, had it not been for our daughters both living on Cape Cod, we might have decided to stay there indefinitely. A simpler life would be almost impossible to find. The enormous quiet of winter and the purity of the water and air was astounding. The quality of friendship would be impossible to replace elsewhere. The forest and water, the hills and the village all beckoned us to stay.

We took our time in provisioning. Looking back, I see that neither of us wanted to go, but we had to go nonetheless. As the days warmed, I knew the time was near. When I finally filled the water tank, I knew there were few excuses left for us to use to prolong our departure. It was June, and things were blooming all around. The birch and poplar trees were in full leaf, and the breezes were warm. The fields were waving with fresh dandelions and tall grass. We had to go.

Nattily Ann was tied to Smith's wharf behind his great tug. Every day we brought things to the boat, but it was the day that Emma made our bunk up that we knew it would be only a short time before departure. The rented cottage was emptied of everything we owned and had accumulated. New books and all the canned goods were loaded on board. We hired a lady to clean and close the cottage and turn in the key for us. Everything was done except for the goodbyes. It was decided that we would have a party for friends and crews at the boat shed. The hotel catered the event with pastries and coffee. Everything was fairly somber until Smith brought out the champagne. With that, everyone's mood was elevated quite a bit. The day ended with Smith and me leaning on the bar we had grown to love so much, singing each other's praises. Smith promised to come and visit us, and oh, how I wish that promise would have come true.

The morning of our departure dawned bright, and the sky was as blue as any sky could be. Our first night on the boat was spent tied to the dock. It was after eight in the morning that we were actually ready to leave. Friends and well-wishers had gathered, and by 9:00 a.m., they were all loaded on the tug to follow us to the locks only a short distance from Smith's dock. Emma wiped tears from her cheek as we rounded the jetty to the locks. With a great blast from the tug's air horn, we waved goodbye forever.

We decided to use the North Channel Canadian locks because that would be the easiest and closest. It would take one day, at least, to leave the St. Marys River, then a two-day sail to the mouth of the St. Clair River, then we would declare our entrance into the United States to the customs office in Detroit. Looking back, the decision to lock through in Canada was an unfortunate one.

The Canadian locks were smaller and less traveled. They were closer, friendlier to the small boat, and cut over an hour off travel time from where we were. Only one man operated the lock, so it was our job to open the floodgates after the water had been dumped out, letting us lower to the next level. The whole deal takes a little under an hour, and then we would be on our way back home. The locks were but a short distance by foot from Smith's dock, and that fact caused fate to turn against me once again. Little did we know that the lowest form of human existence had found me again and was stalking me and my wife, hoping for one more chance to deprive me of my life. It was La Chance who had seen my picture and read the article about the bell in an old discarded paper. Only then did he realize that I wasn't a downcast soul who had robbed him of his chance for freedom. He clearly read that I was a man of means and that I was presiding only a short distance from the cave he had made home while waiting for spring to arrive.

He had caught wind of the fact that my wife and I were sailing back to the east, and in his mind this meant there would be money on board for the trip. He carried his limited thinking to the next step, seeing that a boat would be a great escape vehicle for him. His problem was that he knew nothing about boats or sailing, so if he commandeered my boat, he would have to keep me alive until he found what he was looking for. His hope was to have us take him to the United States, where he could disappear into the crowds and start a new life of debauchery. He was afraid to have his face seen in the little town, so he camped among the piles of firewood behind the water house, where he could watch our movements to and from the boat. What we didn't know was that he would go into the boat at night and steal food and drink. I remember wondering why there was a dirty spoon on our salon table one day, but I just assumed Emma had used it.

There were too many people about on the day that we left, so he cut cross the adjoining coal yard, keeping us in sight until he could see that we were locking through within his reach. He then hid in the bushes only a few feet from the south entrance to the locks and watched Emma tie the boat, while I ground the gates closed some twenty feet above her. If only we had decided to declare on the American side, his plan would have turned to dust.

I closed the lock gates, grinding the gears together until the gates locked tight. Looking down on my boat, I could see my wife secure *Nattily Ann* to the wharf, waiting for me to finish my work. How nice was the sight. Emma waved, and I waved back as I finished rolling those massive doors closed. I skipped down the steps and over to the boat, never thinking that real danger was only fifteen feet away. With dock line in hand, I jumped onto the boat as Emma pushed *Nattily Ann* into gear, and we started off into the river. I was standing there, coiling the dock line, looking forward at the river, when suddenly I heard a loud bang, and then everything went black.

The next thing I knew, I woke from some painfully induced sleep and found myself bound tight with my hands tied behind me. My feet were bare, and I was tied tight at the ankles. What I didn't know was that Armand La Chance had knocked me unconscious as he jumped out from the bushes onto the wharf then onto our boat. He had apparently clobbered me hard with the flat of the gun he had stolen from the Mounty he had beaten so badly during his escape. The cur then pointed the gun at Emma and said that if she made a single sound, he would kill us both. He dragged me down into the salon, where, after stealing my boots and socks, he tied my hands and feet tightly. Then he returned up into the cockpit, pulled his old shoes and worn-out socks off, and tossed them over the side. He put my shoes on his feet and told my wife to do exactly what he said if she cared for her life at all.

He told her that he only wanted money and to be taken to the lower part of Michigan, preferably Detroit. There he promised her he would leave us alone and unharmed if all went according to his plan. She had no idea that this man's very substance was a lie and that he would gladly kill both of us, the only humans who knew of his existence in America. Our fate was sealed the moment he stepped foot on board. Poor Emma panicked. She hid her fear as best she could, having figured out that this was La Chance by his looks and manner, and a very dangerous man indeed. She agreed to pilot the boat down the river and assured him that she would be no trouble. She pleaded for him to let her tend to me. He said no, that he knew I had a gun, and he was going to find it or there would be trouble. Emma knew the situation was critical but had the presence of mind to tell him right away where the gun was. She told him it had a bullet stuck in its barrel and was useless, which she thought was true for I had neglected to tell her the story of the old farmer in an effort to avoid upsetting her.

La Chance found the gun in the bottom of the hanging locker where she had told him it would be but left it there, probably owing to the fact that he already had a gun and was thinking that mine was useless. I was almost sure that he had seen the stuck bullet during our train-board rumble, which was why I think he decided to finish me off then and there and not retrieve the gun as he surely could have done. In fact, the Mounties had joked about the gun, and La Chance never missed a word they said. Emma was surprised to see that he had left it there in the locker. Wisely she avoided any eye contact with this fiend, never offering any comment and always answering "Yes, sir" and "No, sir" in response to his questions, keeping her head lowered.

As I came to, I could vaguely hear voices coming from the cockpit. Once again my head was ringing like that old heavy bell in town. For a brief minute, I thought I might have ended up in the bell tower. I had been hit so hard my vision had doubled and stayed that way for a while. I lay there, straining to hear something. Then I heard the unmistakable voice and surly accent of La Chance. His voice was gruff and dangerous, and all I could do was fear for my wife. What fate was this! Of all the unexpected things to happen! The realization that this was the man who had sworn to kill me struck me like a bullet in the chest. I was hopelessly bound, lying on my cabin floor, and there was a true killer sitting on my very own boat with my wife, and even God didn't know what this man was capable of. Panic-driven scenarios raced through my mind. Visions that remain unspeakable anchored in my thoughts. However would we get out of this? My heart was pounding, and my breath became driven by a real fear for our lives.

Eventually Emma did talk him into letting her check on me. I heard someone coming and, thinking it was La Chance, pretended to still be unconscious. It was my precious wife who embraced me and cried hard tears. "Oh, Shotty, I am so scared." She quivered as she stroked my head.

I tried to focus on her face, but things were still fuzzy for me, so I hoarsely whispered, "Don't worry, sweetheart, I'll think of something."

"Get back up here!" he yelled like a cannon's roar.

"Let him think I am still out while I think of something," I whispered. "Try to keep him in the cockpit, love."

She pulled away from me, looking astounded at the amount of blood that had seeped from the wound on my head onto her hand. She left a bloody hand print on the companionway wall as she climbed the ladder into the cockpit. I heard her let out a yelp, as though she had been struck or something. He had pulled her hair and flung her back to the tiller. The sound of my wife being mistreated like that sent blood into my vision. I struggled hard to free my hands but to no avail. I was furious at this situation. My hands were tied so tight I could feel nothing but pain coming from them. I looked at my feet, and they were turning blue from the lack of blood. If something were to happen to Emma, I would be helpless to do anything at all. In fact, this was a completely hopeless situation that would probably end up with us both dead if I didn't do something and now!

I needed a knife! My rigging knife was in my rucksack but I could never get it out with my hands tied. I knew there was a kitchen knife in the drawer under the sink if I could get to it. If I did it quickly. I found the floor with my tied feet and pushed myself up with my elbows. I managed to stand in a crouch so the top of my head would not be seen from the cockpit. Thank goodness the sound of the engine running fast covered my fumbling about as I tried to find the drawer. I leaned my backside against the cabinet beneath the sink and strained to get my tied hands on the drawer handle. Once I got it open, I blindly felt until I found a small sharp carving knife. It would be easier to conceal if La Chance were to discover my movements.

La Chance stood up in the cockpit, and before he could turn toward the cabin, I closed the drawer and managed to tuck the knife into the back of my pants, beneath my belt. I saw his head and mass of curly hair turning around as I jumped back to where he had left me. It would be hard to pretend to be out, breathing as hard as I was, so I decided to pretend that I was just coming around.

"Reveille!" he shouted at me as he pulled me by my hair, up from the floor to the settee. "Wake up, you bastard!"

I hit the bench hard but had the presence of mind to turn on my back so as not to expose the knife.

"Where is your money?" he shouted in his ugly broken English. "I want your money!" With that, he knocked me to the floor again and viciously stomped me in the face. That I did not like at all, and a hate welled up in me that I had never known before.

"Stop it!" I yelled. "I will show you! Just untie me!"

"Oh no, you will tell me or I will cut off your ear!" he yelled as he pulled a large knife from his sash.

There was no doubt in my mind that he would have done that and worse. The sound of his vicious voice was ringing loudly in the cabin as I looked up from my helpless position at a madman wielding this giant knife menacingly over my face. His voice was like metal grinding against gravel, and the sheer volume sent shots of pain into my ears.

"I only have a little American currency in my rucksack on the forward birth and a few Canadian dollars in my pocket," I almost whimpered as I said this.

With that he reached down and grabbed my pocket, inserted his knife in it, and cut the pocket wide open. The money fell out onto the floor where he grabbed what was there and looked to see it was paltry indeed. He dumped the contents of my rucksack onto the salon table, where he gathered the several hundred dollars I had wrapped up in a rubber band. To my bad fortune, he also saw a book of bank checks from the American Banking Association. There were three of these checks in the amount of one thousand dollars each that were all made out in my wife's name.

"Who is this Emma?" he asked.

I nodded toward the cockpit.

"She can cash these?" was his next question.

I nodded once again. With that, he jumped the steps to the companionway hatch and took a slow look around, locking Emma in his sights. It was the first good look I had of him, and little had changed from our last encounter. He was as close to an animal as a human could get, with an unkempt beard and wild curly hair. He was even wearing some sort of animal skin that was crudely stitched into a vest, with his bare arms sticking out at the shoulders. He stopped looking at Emma, turned in place, and looked down at me. An extremely menacing grin came over his face as he descended the stairs, looking me squarely in the eyes. A more unnerving experience had never come my way as the two of us made that single contact.

"Then you see, I have no further need of you, monsieur!" he said as he effortlessly lifted me fully off the floor and over his shoulder. He carried me up over the hatch, where he threw me into the bottom of the cockpit. Then he stood up and lifted me once again as he got his footing on the edge of the starboard seat. I had no idea what he was up to, but I could see as I looked around that there were no other boats anywhere to be seen on the river. There was nothing around us at all except a small island next to the channel that blocked us from being seen by what little civilization there might be behind us. I looked at Emma and saw raw fear in her eyes. She had never seen anything like this man in her life. She had known of ruffians and seen her father deal with the lowlifes that frequent the docks of the world, but the size and anger in this man was more than she could believe. As our eyes met, I knew this might be the last sight I would ever have of her. Before I could get the words *I love you* out of my mouth, I found myself once again weightless and airborne, having been thrown over the side of the boat.

I felt the pain of my toes hitting the rail of the boat and heard my name screamed in my wife's voice, but then there was nothing but the sounds of the cold water closing in all around me. That sound grew less and less as I felt myself sinking toward the bottom. Then I became aware of the *flap, flap, flap* of the boat's propeller driving away and away and away. I sank and desperately tried to think. I was helplessly entombed in a cold, wet environment with what appeared to be zero options for survival. The knife! I fumbled and grabbed it out of my pants. Thank God it was still there! I managed to get it in my hands and curl my legs up so I could cut the rope on my ankles.

My lungs were starting to feel a searing pain for lack of oxygen, and I knew I had only moments before I would be taking a very final gulp of water.

How strange it was that once again I was at the limits of my abilities. If I could not free my feet, these would be my last moments here on this earth, and that thought alone forced me past my limits once again. I sawed and sawed on that rope as hard as I could with a knife I could not see, on a rope I could not feel.

It worked! The rope was cut, and my feet struggled free. I kicked furiously until my face, eyes, and nose came free from that drowning river. I gulped one breath of fresh air and then began another descent toward the bottom. As I sank, I quieted myself enough to concentrate on cutting my hands free with the knife held inverted awkwardly between two fingers. It was hard because my hands were behind me and it took endless moments, but it worked! I was free again! My fingers were numb with pain from the contortion it took to slice through the rope. With searing lungs, I swam to the surface, one hand tightly clutching the little knife. Aside from my wits, it was my only weapon, and swimming was my only salvation. I was shaking violently from adrenaline and cold as I pulled myself toward a little island in the middle of the river. Once I got my footing on the bottom, I wasted little time in running over the spit to the other side, where I could see my boat in the distance with La Chance at the tiller. There was no sight of Emma and nothing in the water behind the boat that might have been the result of him throwing her over too. Of course he wouldn't throw her overboard, I thought; he needed her to cash the thousand-dollar checks. The nearest place he could get them cashed would be Alpena, Michigan, only about seventy miles to the south, where there was a bank. He didn't know that there was a bank there, and even if he did, I doubted if he even knew how to cash a check. One thing I did know was that if he started asking Emma questions, she would quickly figure it out.

I knew Emma wouldn't tell him that they could stop in Alpena, if she even knew about the checks. It would only mean she would die sooner if she didn't think this thing out. I knew she would rather take her chances in Detroit, where she might be able to escape or get help.

I trusted Emma to do the right thing, but I could not be sure that she could stay ahead of this fiend. I had to catch them!

The current was moving at about two knots at that point, and my boat would be cruising at another four knots, making them pull away from me at six knots. Another problem I had was that the little sand spit I was on was on the Canadian side of the river. If I wanted to catch up, I would have to get to the American side fast. It would have been over a mile if I swam straight across, and I wasn't sure if I could make it. I elected to straddle two small logs and attempt to cross the river while riding its current south. Within half an hour, I had two driftwood logs of similar size under me, and I was paddling as hard as I could with my hands. My thighs became so tired from trying to hold the logs together that I slid into the cold water between them and propelled myself by kicking while my arms held me up as much as possible. In what seemed like a couple of hours, I had seen no boats, but I could see a road on the Michigan side where an occasional car or truck went by. The road was close to the riverbank but very far away from me. With each anxious moment, I grew more impatient and tired.

It appeared that I was getting farther away from the road rather than closer to it, so I decided to abandon the logs and swim. That way I would be less influenced by the current but more exposed to the cold water. Looking back, it was a foolish decision. Swim I did. I dog-paddled and breast-stroked. I floated on my back when I could swim no more. I was numb with cold and began to doubt the wisdom of leaving the logs behind. I must have only been a few hundred feet from the shore when my power all but gave out. I had nothing left. I thought about the escape from my island prison so many months past. I never would have swum this far in such cold water as that was. This water was warmer than Lake Superior, but still I had no strength left to fight it. I felt that I could not catch my breath and feared that my heart might give out. All I could do to stay alive was to abandon my plan of getting to the road and just try to tread water until I could rest and find another way out.

Many years at sea had taught me the various methods of surviving in any water. I had only once in my life at sea been forced to take to the water, and that was the time our pulling boat shipped a wave and sank off the coast of Honduras. She went down in a flash and left us nothing to grab or hold on to, because we had only round casks of fresh water that would barely float themselves. My crew of three and I were forced to swim for the better part of an hour trying to get back to the beach we had just left. We were rescued by sundown when the seas subsided. The water temperature was very tolerable in those latitudes, not to mention that I was twenty-five years younger.

I stopped swimming and began to kick myself upright to change my pace from swimming to simply treading water if I could. As I did so, my toes hit something solid. At first I thought I had hit a fish or turtle or something. Then I realized I was touching a sandy, muddy bottom! I had inadvertently come upon a sand bar where I could stand and regain my strength! Once again an angel had held my hand, and I had been pulled from a life-threatening situation into a very good, lifesaving situation. I stood there in chest deep water for many anxious but rehabilitating minutes, though I had to fight for my footing in the current. It was then that I realized I was way out of the channel, and it was possible the bottom might be close to the surface all the way to land. It was, though muddy to the calves in some places, and I made it to the bank exhausted and ready to give up, but I knew I could not quit now. My wife's very life depended on me finding help and getting to her soon. That thought drove me onward, losing all sense of time and distance.

I hit a deep patch of water close to the grassy shore, so I pushed off and swam the last five hundred feet. Pulling my exhausted body up on the bank, I rolled onto my back and tried to absorb sunlight to warm my freezing extremities. I could feel its warmth on my face, and as I lay there, I might have slipped into sleep for a while. I could hear the blood from my overworked heart rushing through my ears, and my head ached still from the blow I had received at the hands of Armand La Chance. As I regained my strength to a point, I rolled over on my belly to gaze toward where I knew there would be a road. The question was, once I made it to the road, even if I could get a ride, should I go back to Sault Ste. Marie and get help, or should I try going south and find help that way?

The sun was getting low, and I felt almost sure that they would have to stop somewhere down river because of the many shoals and the lack of navigation lights on the river. Anchoring out of the channel would be the only option before not being able to travel farther in the diminished light. I could only imagine what horrors my wife might be subjected to at the hands of that man. One thing I did know was that he needed her and would not harm her until he had the money in his big grubby hands. She was a savvy woman and knew the water as well or better than I did. I felt sure I could anticipate her moves if she had control of the boat. She would delay their progress much as possible if she could.

Further south there were no towns to stop at except at the very mouth of the river, so they would have to anchor outside of the channel somewhere between here and the open water of Lake Huron. I elected to go south and stick to road and the bank in hopes of sighting them. After all, La Chance had no idea I was still alive. Somehow I would find help, but I knew that I should not let them get too far ahead of me no matter what. My hopes were that the angel that had been watching over me would not let me down now. I elected to attempt the rescue myself and headed south.

What I suspected but didn't really know was that Emma was completely distraught. She thought she had seen the man she loved thrown to his death in the cold river water. La Chance had slapped her hard repeatedly and pulled her hair to get her to stop crying. She leaped down into the cabin and threw herself onto the floor, still wet with my blood. Emma knew absolutely that she was in danger of meeting my fate and vowed to stay alive to mete revenge on this man and see her daughters once again. She decided to play the dumb, foolish woman and take her chance for escape whenever it arrived.

La Chance enjoyed the time alone in the cockpit, steering the boat without a screaming woman bothering him. It became obvious however that he knew nothing about what he was doing when he ran the boat onto a sandbar well outside the clearly marked channel. He yelled for Emma to come topside and see what was the matter. When she did so, she realized he didn't know how to run a boat and that she would be safe as long as he needed her. This knowledge gave her hope in her time of despair. She finally had some control, though very little, and she might be able to use it to her advantage. Unfortunately she still had no knowledge of the thousand-dollar checks being his ultimate goal. Emma was under the impression at the time that he needed her only to help him run the boat and that she was expendable other than that. She used her knowledge of the sea to rock the boat against the current until she freed the boat from the sandy bottom.

It was then that she told him she would behave and be of no trouble. She feared for her life and safety. Fear of this vicious man clouded her thinking somewhat, and as a result, she became quite timid. All she could think of then was seeing her daughters again. With fear as her motivation, she never lowered her vigilance, constantly looking for a window of opportunity. His answer was to warn her that he would take no backtalk, and he shouted for her to get him some food. She did as he asked, and as she reentered the cockpit, she quietly warned him that the light was getting dim, and they would have to be out of the channel within the hour or risk the chance of being run down by a freighter or otherwise wrecking the boat. He was reluctant to allow anyone to make decisions for him, but even this fool understood that Emma K. Murphy knew what she was doing.

Freight-bearing ships move fast in those waters, especially going south, and do not stop for the night. Instead they used large, powerful searchlights to find their way through the channels. Smaller boats must stay out of their way. Just the wake from one of these monsters can cause damage to a small boat if one is not careful. Emma had chosen a stopping spot as close to shore as she could safely get. She hoped that maybe she could jump into the water and swim to shore, but La Chance had a different idea. As soon as the anchor was down, he cruelly threw her down below, where he tied her as tight as he had tied me. He threw her into the forward birth and admonished her to stay put and be quiet. She asked what to do if she had to go to the bathroom, and his reply was to go where she lies. From the smell of him, one would surmise that was what he did on a regular basis.

Before he left the forepeak, he untied her boots and removed them from her feet, throwing the boots into the cabin. He stood there staring at her feet for all too many uncomfortable moments. Emma felt a fear so foreign to her it was a surprise. She had never feared for her virtue before, and at that time, she was naked to the world for all intents and purposes, with only two light hemp ropes between her and the ravages of this monster. That night this monster, who had injected his murderous self into our lives, found the bottle of Canadian whisky that Smith had given me as a going away gift. He drank from it freely and sat on the bunk in the salon, grunting and mumbling like the pig he was, feeding himself with anything he found to shove in his face. He was getting drunk and shouting insults at my wife. The drunker he got, the worse they were. At one point he went forward and stared at her for another uncomfortable time, with only his silhouette visible in the cabin lantern's light. Emma pretended to be sleeping, but that night she slept only a little. Her fear of what this man might do was well warranted.

Not one of several vehicles that passed me stopped that evening. I was covered in mud, barefoot, and water soaked, with my front pocket hanging open. I had no money or identification on me. After the sun went down, I had to keep walking on the road just to stay warm. I could not get dry in the night mist and wished for a match to build a fire while I waited for morning. That night was as miserable as any I had spent on this earth. I finally stopped walking and sat by the side of the road with a makeshift pine-bough lean-to over my head to ward off the dew and cold. It wasn't until daybreak that my luck took hold, and a truck pulled to a stop. It was a farmer taking his cans of milk to a drop-off point. As I got into his truck, he whistled and told me I looked like hell. "Did you fall off o' one of them freighters?" was his question.

I asked him if he would mind turning up his heater then told him my story and asked him to take me as far as he could. He knew the river well and helped his brother fish the lakes in the summer, but he couldn't remember if the road stayed next to the riverbank the whole way. That wasn't his usual route south. I could tell the farmer thought I was crazy, but when I mentioned that I had left Sault Ste.

Marie, Canada, that previous morning. He laughed and told me about a story he had read about a boy who was lifted off the ground up there by a falling bell. I told him that what he had read about was my project, and when he heard that news, he turned toward me and switched on his dome light to see that I was the man pictured in the article. That realization added some urgency to his tone.

"You are in trouble!" he said as if he had doubted my sanity before.

"That's what I've been saying!" I said.

"There ain't no cops around these parts, but I can take you to my brother's house, where his boat is tied up. Maybe he can be of some help." His words had the air of apology.

Thank Goodness someone was there to help. The ride was filled with endless questions from the old farmer. I talked him into turning up the cab heater, which began to thaw me out. I would hear his words streaming along without understanding one of them, but the warmth of the heater was making me drowsy, and I couldn't fight the urge to fall asleep in fits and starts. It took about an hour to get to his brother's house, and he was still sleeping when we arrived. The farmer, John Marshall, introduced me to his brother, Sigrid, and wasted no time telling him my story. Sigrid stood in his kitchen, heating water for some kind of hot drink, and listened to his brother John's and my tale.

Luck had turned her face toward me once again. Sigrid owned a motor-driven fishing boat that was completely enclosed, as is the style for lake fishing boats. These boats go out all year-round and needed the protection from the elements. It was tied to some posts sticking out of the river and was awaiting the beginning of the commercial fishing season. I saw it sitting there in the dawning light and knew that this could possibly be Emma's salvation. Normally, Sigrid would take the boat down river to a fishery where he would spend most of his summer fishing. The season was just over a week away, but the boat was ready now. I asked him if he would take me down to the lake, where I might just spot my boat and find a way to rescue my wife. He explained that he worked at the sawmill on the night shift and was very much afraid of losing his job if he didn't show up, but he did consent to rent the boat to me after some real begging and many promises to pay by me. His brother assured him that I was good for it, having read the article and spotting me as the moneyman.

"This guy don't look it Sigrid, but I read in the paper that he has got plenty of money, and I feel we can trust him," Old John reassured his brother. John Marshall was looking out for me. He talked his brother into renting me his boat and even wrote up a little contract on a brown paper bag for me to sign. The boat was full of gas and ready to go, so I shook each fellow's hand and got an agreement from John that he would call the authorities as soon as he was near a phone.

Sigrid ran after me as I stepped on the plank to board his boat and gave me pair of old work boots, a worn-out old sweater, and an old sawed-off shotgun with some shells that he had obviously had for a long time. "They ain't much, but they are better'n what you got," he said.

He showed me the trick to starting the boat and sent me off with a stout "Good luck!"

These were good men, and I would be back to reward them sooner than they thought. I hoped the shotgun and the few shells he gave me would help save the day, but I could take no chances that might endanger my wife's life. They both gave me a shove into the current with the end of a plank and waved as I put the boat into gear and pulled into the river.

The boat *Lucky Gal* was about twenty-eight to thirty feet long, and she did have a good motor in her. It was a straight-six Chrysler Crown that had much more power than *Nattily Ann*'s motor did. I figured it would do at least eight knots without straining her too much. The question was, where was *Nattily Ann*? I didn't know exactly where I was and wasn't sure if she was in front of me or behind me. I did my best to calculate. It was after 11:00 a.m. when I was thrown into the water, and the sun went down at about 7:30 p.m. or so. That meant they had traveled around thirty or thirty-five miles, which would put them only an hour or so from Lake Huron. What I didn't know was that I was about two hours from Point de Tours

Village, which was the last stopping point before the river spilled into Lake Huron. I had no choice once I reached the open lake but to set a course for Detroit and hope that I could catch up with them before I ran out of gas.

Sigrid's charts were new and much better than the ones on my boat. I finally figured where I was by reading the numbers on the channel markers. I didn't know just how close I was to *Nattily Ann* or that they had spent the better part of two hours aground or that Emma had anchored well before dark. I had no plan, but I knew that La Chance had a gun and a knife, and he would not hesitate to use either of them. He had tried to kill me twice already and would do the same to anyone who got in his way, including, perish the thought, my precious wife.

Point De Tour Village came in sight at about 10:45 a.m., and there were several ships and smaller boats in the area. A giant ship carrying iron ore, probably from Minnesota south to Cleveland or Chicago, passed me. I watched it go on as it passed a sailboat farther down river and then out into the open waters of Lake Huron. I lifted the binoculars Sigrid had on his chart table and watched the ship take a turn to the left, which meant it wouldn't be going to Chicago. Then I panned down and looked at the sailboat it had just passed. It was *Nattily Ann*! My heart leapt up into my throat, and my hands instantly started sweating. She was too far from me to see who was at the helm. The boat was about a mile and one-half away, heading straight out into the lake. I could tell it was my ship by the rig and shape of the hull; there was no mistaking it! Instinctively I pushed the throttle all the way forward feeling a slight surge in speed. Truly that did nothing, for the boat was already at its top speed.

My thoughts were on just how I was going to get my wife off that boat unharmed. The greatest advantage I had was that La Chance would not suspect that he was being followed by a dead man. He could not see who was in the fishing tug because it was closed in all around, and the little tug was faster than the sailboat. I had to get close enough to see what was going on without drawing attention to me. I followed behind, getting close enough within half an hour to see that it was Emma alone at the helm. What I didn't know was

La Chance had bound her tightly to the tiller in such a way that she could not get loose. As I closed in, I did not see the villain anywhere. I was as nervous as anyone could get. How would I deal with this giant man who seemed to have no end to his strength?

It seems La Chance had a hangover and had gone down for a nap after he had seen that they were safely out in the lake. Of course, Emma did not know she was being followed by me when she boldly decided to take advantage of his sleeping and changing their course to the west. She could hear him snoring over the sound of the motor and had hoped to be able to run the boat aground in the busy harbor at Mackinac Island and either jump to freedom or scream for help before the lout realized what was happening. It was a desperate plan and would only work if he slept for much more than just one hour.

I was puzzled at first, but then I saw that she was making straight for the island. The problem was that she hadn't realized that, at full throttle, the boat had used almost all its available gasoline. The little engine was smoking and steaming, but she kept it wide open, hoping to cut her time to the island as much as she could. I closed to within two hundred feet alongside. She looked over at the *Lucky Gal* and assumed that it was just returning to the island with a load of fish. At about one hundred feet abreast of her, I stood on the pilot's seat and pushed the hatch above my head open, sticking the top half of my body out. For well over a half minute, she stared at me waving at her until it registered that it was me and I was still alive. I saw her happily try to stand and then fall back because of the ropes. She couldn't take her eyes off me and almost steered into my boat. Her smile was as large as the horizon, and I am sure it was the first time fear had left her for even a moment.

Waving my hands in a downward motion, I signaled for her to slow the boat down. She had the presence of mind to do it slowly enough so as not to wake La Chance. My plan was to get over to her, get on that boat, cut her free, and escape from La Chance on the fishing tug. As we each slowed, the two boats converged. When I was close enough to loudly whisper for her to go into neutral, she did just that. Both boats were closing at a fast drift when I jumped out of the hatch and quietly boarded *Nattily Ann* with the little kitchen knife in my mouth.

I cut her hands loose and told her to steer into the tug. Just as I bent to cut her legs free, the sailboat's engine backfired and quit, running out of gas right then and there. The backfire was enough to wake the sleeping giant and send him dashing to the ladder. I turned just in time to see his enormous head coming up the steps. Instinctively, in that life-threatening situation, I thrust out with the knife and stuck it squarely into his neck just below his left ear. He shoved me violently back with his right hand and let out a scream that could have been heard in Chicago. He reeled and pulled at the knife sticking into his neck. It must have struck a bone or hooked one or something, because it appeared that the knife was truly stuck there. He tugged on the knife handle and roared with the pain that it gave him, still unable to dislodge it from his neck. He looked at me with red fiery eyes that would have frightened the very devil himself. Though the knife was small, it caused him considerable discomfort.

Emma had freed herself and made an incredible leap over to the tug, where she now stood screaming my name. As I turned to look at her, La Chance managed to grab me by the back of the shirt with a force that almost ripped it off my body. Once again he threw me to the cockpit floor. I was not going to stay there while he finished climbing out of the cabin. I made an attempt to jump for my life when he grabbed me again. This time he lifted me straight up, shaking me with ease, the whole time growling like a wild animal, and then flung me right down the stairs into the cabin, where there was no hope for escape. I saw him lift his massive leg over the threshold and start down into the cabin again. Behind him I could see Emma was back on the boat, standing and shouting something I could not hear over his roars. Then I heard her say, "Your gun, Shotty. Your gun!"

That was it! My gun was just inches away in the locker. I frantically opened the locker and grabbed the gun. Just above it on a shelf was a box of bullets, and I thrust my hand into it, retrieving only one bullet. I jammed it immediately into the chamber, spun the chamber to where I thought the shell would hit the barrel, and cocked the thing just in time to find La Chance upon me. La Chance saw me aiming what he thought was a useless gun square at his heart. He stopped in his tracks for a moment, and then that horrible grin started over his face again. It was obvious that he was thinking this was the same trick I had tried to pull on him on the train. Once again, he began to come closer to my trembling pistol.

This was it! The moment of truth was at hand, and I slowly squeezed the trigger. The hammer fell on an empty chamber, and all that was heard was a loud metallic click. The noise caused La Chance to stop in his tracks for a moment. This time he looked closer at the gun, and the intimidating smile disappeared from his face. He could see that there was no longer a bullet lodged in my gun's barrel, and then he saw the chamber spin a bullet to the barrel as I squeezed once again. The recoil of the shot almost broke my wrist. The sound was deafening, and the smoke was acrid and everywhere in the cabin. I could hear Emma screaming over the ringing in my ears. I saw the massive hulk of a man trying to climb the steps, struggling with every move. I had shot him at close range and hit him in the left breast, just below the shoulder. It was the first time I had ever fired that gun, and I had shot a man with it!

Reaching into the locker, I quickly filled the chamber with five more bullets. The injured man had crawled out into the cockpit and was attempting to stand, but the shock of being shot was too much for him. He was pale and moaning, the knife still protruding from his neck. His right hand was pressed over the wound, but it was doing little to stop the blood from finding its way out. I stood there on the deck and looked around. Emma was staring at him with her hand covering her mouth, as if to suppress more screams. I looked over the water, and aside from a silver-painted fishing tug floating near us, there was no one out there to come to our aid. I knew by the amount of blood coming from the bullet hole that La Chance's wounds were not mortal, and for a moment I thought about finishing him off but then was disgusted with the thought of it. We would have to get to a harbor where the police could take over. It would have to be soon, the way he was bleeding, because I would do nothing to stem his bleeding myself. From now on, the bastard was on his own.

La Chance looked up at me one-eyed, from the side of his face. He knew he was beaten, but I could not trust him to lie still. I yelled at him to get up and go down below. I knew we could lock him there and tow the boat to a safe harbor. He said something like "Go to hell," but I would not take it. I put the pistol down close to his ear and pulled the trigger sending a bullet through the cockpit bridge right next to his left hand. Emma screamed again, but this time it was my name.

"I know what I'm doing, Emma!" I yelled back.

La Chance rose and clumsily fell down into the cabin. I opened the lazarette, retrieved the hatch boards, and pushed them into place, never letting go of the gun. I pulled the hatch closed and slid the lock into the hasp, locking our murderous intruder below. The forward hatch was way too small for his girth to get through, so for the first time in over twenty-four hours, I felt safe. Floating there in the windless, lazy sea with only the sound of the fishing tug's motor breaking the silence, Emma and I stood embracing each other, alternately crying and laughing. We had survived! We had beaten every obstacle put in front of us and found ourselves back together again, safe and alive!

As I looked into her beautiful brown eyes, I lifted my face to the sky and shouted, "My god, what an adventure this has been!"

I managed to scull the rudder enough to fetch the tug, which we tied tightly alongside and then pushed into gear, using the tug's power for propulsion and the sailboat's rudder to steer us back toward Point de Tour, just five miles away. We could hear La Chance calling to us from below, but to be honest, we didn't care if he made it or not.

John Marshall had done well. He had contacted the police and was on board the local rescue boat that approached us when we were but a few miles out from de Tour. They pulled alongside and shouted over to us, and we yelled back and forth, trying to figure what to do with our cargo. Apparently, there was a police car back at the dock with a radio in it, but the nearest ambulance was in St. Ignace, over thirty miles away. I told them to get back there and call for it but to make sure there were plenty of extra men around to hold this man down. As they started to pull off, I yelled across to John, saying, "John, I am not kidding! Bring as many men as you can!"

There was much activity as we pulled alongside the wharf, including two police cars and many onlookers. I guided the tug in slowly and touched *Nattily Ann* to the dock very lightly. There was a lot of help tying her up, then a quiet came over the crowd as a horrible screeching, groaning, yelling sound was heard from below. Everyone was silently looking at the hatch when suddenly there was a loud crashing sound pounding right up through it. La Chance was pounding the hatch with the fire extinguisher, I supposed, and was having some success destroying my boat. The thought of this sent me into a rage, and without thinking about it, I picked up my revolver and fired two shots in succession right up into the air. Everyone either flung themselves to the ground or began running away with that, but they stopped when they heard me yell at the hatch, "The next one is for you, you murdering, stinking lowlife scum!" This stopped the pounding almost immediately.

As I looked at all the surprised faces around me, I began to laugh. None of these people had any idea what was down in that hole, and if they had, they wouldn't have been standing around here. Any sane person would be as far away from this monster as they could be. He was responsible for the deaths of how many persons, no one knew, but two of them were his own grandparents! He was capable of living in trees or in caves or on the ground while waiting for a victim to walk along, and I wouldn't have been the slightest bit surprised if he had eaten some of his victims as well. This man was the poorest example of the human spirit alive and was a vile and loathsome creature indeed.

Emma started laughing as she watched me standing there in my torn and muddy clothes. The sight of her peaceful husband in that condition, standing on our boat, pointing my smoking gun at our boat's cabin in anger, just broke her up. She too knew who this man was and found humor in the crowd's reaction. They thought we were the crazy ones instead of our cargo!

The sheriff of Chippewa County came on board and began to ask me what had transpired. My words were slow to come out, probably owing to exhaustion. He had no idea what to think, having already heard Marshall's version. I did my best to explain the series of events but virtually gave up, telling him to contact the Canadian authorities because they wanted this man badly. I put my hand on his arm as he wrote my words with a pencil into a small notebook, and when I had his attention, I remember just what I said.

"Sheriff, we have a very, very dangerous man here, and even though he is wounded with a knife and gunshot, he is still capable of killing you and everyone around you, so please be careful."

He looked at me as if I were insane. The question on his face was overridden by his knowledge that he was the lawman here. "We'll be just fine, Mr. Murphy. Thank you for your concern."

With that, the sheriff called for his men and asked me to open the hatch. I could see everyone tensing and moving back, including my wife, as I undid the lock and started to pull the hatch boards. Once the hatch was open, I moved back so the sheriff could do his job. With his sidearm drawn, he stepped in front of the hatch, looked into the dark hole, and shouted, "Come on out with your hands up!"

At almost the moment he finished saying those words, there was a flame and a loud blast that came from below. *Blam!* La Chance had shot the sheriff. I had forgotten that La Chance had the gun that he had taken from the Canadian constable, and he had used it to shoot the sheriff! How could I have forgotten his gun! Sheriff Dan Carpenter fell backward with his wide brimmed hat going over before him, right into the cockpit. Another shot rang out and apparently hit nothing. I was on my knees on the seat next to the sheriff when I unconsciously raised my gun up into the hatchway and unloaded it into the cabin. *Blam! Blam! Blam! Blam!* My word, that old Navy .45 was loud! After I stopped firing the gun, I could barely hear La Chance screaming, "Okay! Okay! Okay!"

By this time, the sheriff was sitting up, holding his bleeding ear, which La Chance had shot half off. His gun hand was shaking like a leaf in a windstorm, so I took his gun from him, knowing that mine was empty, and I might need his to do more shooting. Looking over to that wide-eyed lawman, I could see he needed help to get to his feet. With blood running down his cheek, he cautiously took another look into the cabin and saw that I had got La Chance once again. This time I had gotten him in the thigh. The sheriff's other men were standing at hand with guns drawn and what looked like a pile of tire-chains in their hands. I leaned over and yelled for La Chance to throw out his weapon and come out or he would never live to regret it. The gun popped out onto the deck, but he yelled up at us that he couldn't move. I yelled back at him that I was going to start shooting if he didn't come up right now, so there he was, crawling up out of the cabin. Sheriff Carpenter couldn't believe my boldness had worked so well.

Everyone was surprised to see the size of this man as he laboriously pulled himself from the cabin. He ponderously pulled himself along with his enormous arms. Those arms were as big as tree trunks, and as he pulled himself over to the seat, I could see that six-inch knife was still sticking out of his neck with surprisingly little blood seeping from the wound. He had two bullets in him and a knife sticking in his neck, only inches from a major artery, but I knew that this man was still very dangerous. A man I assumed was a medic wrapped his bleeding wounds there on the boat, and they were just trying to get him to stand when the ambulance arrived. I gave the sheriff his gun as well as the gun that La Chance had shot him with.

The sheriff stood there with his large western-style hat on top of his bandaged head, looking at me like I was the biggest mystery of his life.

The sheriff did thank me though, in a manner that made me know he was feeling good to be alive. That made three of us. Emma, Dan Carpenter, and I had all had a close call at the hands of an insane man, and we all knew just how good it was to still be alive. With sweet Emma at my side, we watched as four men struggled to lift the gurney with that giant man on it into the ambulance. We watched as it drove away with the police in parade. I don't know how Emma actually felt right then, but for me, I felt as if life was beginning all over. I looked at my wife then back to the boat and asked her if she wanted to check in to a hotel for a couple of days. I don't need to tell you what her answer was.

Several days later, after we had paid someone to have the boat cleaned, we went to look at it. The blood had been scrubbed away, and except for some errant bullet holes and splintered wood, she was in good order. I must admit, we rented a car from the Ford dealership in town and did some touring for a while, which we found very relaxing. We had the *Lucky Gal* cleaned also then left her at the fishery dock with one of Emma's checks made out to John and Sigrid Marshall left on the chart table, under the binoculars. I felt sure that those gentlemen's trust in me warranted this reward. Emma followed me in the rented Mercury as I delivered *Lucky Gal* with a full tank of gas and the reward money to the Gale Brothers Fisheries just three miles from the town.

For many nights after the incident, Emma found no solid sleep. She became prone to outbursts of loud talking that interrupted what had otherwise been peaceful slumber. I slept little also. Ugly thoughts haunted us both and spilled into the day. For two days we mentioned nothing about the boat or La Chance. I never asked her what had transpired between them and know only what it was she wanted to tell me. As the days went by and we had rested ourselves well, we returned to the boat to survey the damage once again. I was afraid that neither of us would ever want to return to sea at all. I honestly put *Nattily Ann* out of my thoughts, as if she were responsible for our terror. It didn't seem right that such a beautiful boat should remain unattended on the barren quay at Point De Tour. It was as if we had to forgive her for our trouble, but as we stood there looking at her, the memories of bad things began to fall away. We could see that she was none the worse for the trial, so why should we be? Emma and I vowed there and then to leave this place and forget the troubles that we were allowing to haunt us.

This we did, and within one week of our tribulation, we were again underway. This time our departure was quiet as we slipped out into the cold blue waters of Lake Huron, unnoticed by anyone. We had made very few acquaintances in Point de Tour, but the citizens there never noticed us. Our sunrise departure was somber, and for the life of me, I don't remember anything that was said between us until we hit the St. Clair River.

It must have been another week before I noticed that we were laughing again. The ring of our laughing in unison stopped us both from what we were doing. The realization of the moment gave us heart. We had survived, and we had each other. The world was ours, but better yet, we belonged to the world. The trip back home held little excitement in comparison to our first two days, but we did see many wondrous sights.

As I passed the human population of this planet while we traveled, I found no more strangers. My adventures had taught me that I was brother to many, and all I had to do to earn that position was to be a friend, no matter what it took. People who didn't even know me, and who might have found reason to doubt me if they did, helped me without reservation. These people gave me something no book or preacher could hand over. A good heart is the footpath for love, and love is the salvation of man. It takes a lifetime of trials to harden a man. It took just one life-threatening adventure to open his eyes. My boat had turned out to be my best teacher, and in fact, the boat had turned out to be my best friend.

The story I relate to you took shape in my mind on that voyage home, and though many years have passed and I have almost no time for the sea these days, my beautiful boat silently waits at her mooring in case the urge should overtake me to find something that may lie over the horizon. When the time is right and the sweet sounds and smells of the sea beckon, God himself could find no greater pleasure. He provided us with this entire world for our use, and one could find no more wondrous satisfaction than that which is given by wind, wave, and sail.

The End

About the Author

Richard "Dick" Thomas Coleman is a product of being born during the Second World War in 1943. Living and growing up in Milwaukee, a predominantly German community, gave Coleman a more worldly approach to dealing with humanity. Joining the working world at an early age and setting off on the road to adventure, Coleman acquired a wide range of knowledge and obtained a pilot's license at age eighteen and flying military-related freight during the Vietnam War, into Chicago's O'Hare, one of the busiest airports in the world.

He also received his captain license at an early age and found the lure of the seas compelling. Finding great joy in the art of teaching others to sail and operate boats while making a living at it compelled Coleman to journal his experiences at sea, leading him into the art of storytelling and honing his love of writing.

CPSIA information can be obtained
at www.ICGtesting.com
Printed in the USA
LVHW072333280419
615901LV00022B/403/P